DRAGON'S PLUNDER

Books in the Dragonflight Series

LETTERS FROM ATLANTIS
by Robert Silverberg

THE DREAMING PLACE
by Charles de Lint

THE SLEEP OF STONE
by Louise Cooper

BLACK UNICORN
by Tanith Lee

CHILD OF AN ANCIENT CITY
by Tad Williams and Nina Kiriki Hoffman

DRAGON'S PLUNDER
by Brad Strickland

DRAGON'S PLUNDER

Brad Strickland

Illustrated by
Wayne D. Barlowe

A Byron Preiss Book

Atheneum 1992 New York
Maxwell Macmillan Canada
Toronto

Maxwell Macmillan International
New York   Oxford   Singapore   Sydney

DRAGON'S PLUNDER
Dragonflight Books

DRAGON'S PLUNDER copyright © 1992 by Byron Preiss Visual
Publications, Inc.

Text copyright © 1992 by Brad Strickland
Illustrations copyright © 1992 by Byron Preiss Visual
Publications, Inc.

Cover painting by Wayne D. Barlowe
Book design by Paula Keller and Linda Roppolo
Book edited by David M. Harris

Special thanks to Jonathan Lanman, David Keller,
and John Betancourt

Atheneum
Macmillan Publishing Company
866 Third Avenue, New York, NY 10022

Maxwell Macmillan Canada, Inc.
1200 Eglinton Avenue East
Suite 200
Don Mills, Ontario M3C 3N1
First Edition
Printed in the United States of America
10 9 8 7 6 5 4 3 2 1

Library of Congress Cataloging-in-Publication Data

Strickland, Brad.
        Dragon's plunder
              p.   cm.
        Summary: Having been kidnapped by former pirates because of his
ability to whistle up the wind, fifteen-year-old Jamie agrees to
help their leader, a living corpse, find the dragon of Windrose
Island.
        ISBN 0-689-31573-2
        [1. Dragons—Fiction. 2. Pirates—Fiction. 3. Fantasy.]
        I. Title.
        PZ7.S9166Dr   1992
        [Fic]—dc20   91–45664

Because a promise is a promise,
this book is dedicated with love
to the students and teachers
of Myers School,
and to the memory
of Mr. Dean Myers

# CHAPTER 1

At the Pirate's Rest

Jamie Falconer, half run off his feet by the demands of the inn's customers, was probably the last person in the Pirate's Rest to notice the stranger. The man stood framed in the doorway with bright afternoon light behind him, an exceedingly thin fellow of about fifty, with curly black hair just going silver and tied in a pigtail in back, a long-jawed face, two brooding dark blue eyes, and a prominent nose. He wore a purple broadcloth greatcoat, old but clean and neatly brushed, and his boots, though broken in from long service, were well greased and supple.

In his right hand the stranger carried a black walking stick, nicely lacquered and crowned with a yellowish white handle of sea ivory. He raised the cane and aimed its silvery ferrule at Jamie. "You, potboy."

Jamie swallowed hard at the sound of the deep, musical voice, wondering if some rich gentleman, perhaps gifted with a marvelous magical talent, had come by coach and six down the King's Highway from Newberry. But as he set the tray of mugs down on a counter and approached the man he caught a whiff of the sea: tobacco, rum, honest sweat, and salt all compounded together. "Yes, sir?"

The man lowered his cane. "Is your master about?"

"In the kitchen, sir."

The stranger nodded. "Very good. Go tell him that Mr. Pye,

1

first mate of the good ship *Betty*, wants a word with him. Take this for your trouble." The man produced a silver coin and extended it to Jamie on his long, thin palm.

Jamie gulped. "I can't accept it, sir. Why, it's as much as my master allows me in a year!"

"Take it you shall," the man said, and somehow he put the coin into Jamie's hand.

Jamie stared at the unexpected treasure. It was a silver clymento, with a strange monarch's face on one side and an ornate star on the other, and the words stamped on it were foreign. Jamie knew it had to come from Britolak or perhaps from one of the outlandish island countries on the Zampish Main.

He backed away, grinning his pleasure. From his perch beside the door, Squok the parrot whistled a warning, too late for Jamie to react. The boy collided with a fat, soft belly, encased in a great white apron.

The belly's owner pinched Jamie's left ear hard enough to bring water to his eyes. "Ouch!" He squirmed. "Mr. Growdy, this gentleman wants to see you—"

"Oh, does he?" growled Mr. Phineas Growdy, the owner of the inn. With a last pinch he let Jamie go. "And what's your business, stranger?"

For a moment Mr. Pye did not answer, but a flicker of temper showed deep in his dark blue eyes. "Come and see." He stepped back, and Growdy and Jamie followed him to the innyard.

The Pirate's Rest stood on a grassy hill overlooking the village of Gunnel Bay, and through the intervening yews, elms, larches, and houses Jamie could see the harbor, shimmering with the light of the lowering sun. A soft western breeze came off it, bringing the smells of fish and tar. Mr. Pye pointed again with his cane. "You see the ship *Betty* in the harbor there. She is loading provisions and undergoing some light repairs at present. Her master, Captain Octavius Deadmon, desires that I arrange with you for the accommodation of eight men for one week. I suppose you have a sufficient number of rooms?"

Growdy rubbed his unshaven jowls, making a papery sound.

"I ain't got room-stretchin' magic—this here be a country inn, not a fancy hotel—but if they don't mind sleepin' two to a room, I can fit 'em in."

"Good. The cost of the rooms and meals?"

"A week, says you? Well, I can put up eight men for a week and board 'em for, oh—" Growdy cleared his throat, squinted at Pye craftily, and rumbled, "Say, a gulden."

Pye gave Growdy a long look. After a moment he thrust his hand into the bosom of his greatcoat and produced a leather purse. He shook from it a gold coin, a shiny new King Carleton gulden, and gave it to Growdy. "Done."

Growdy looked stunned as he regarded the coin gleaming on his palm. Then he coughed. "Ah—drink is extry."

"I understand." Mr. Pye smiled. "Perfectly."

Jamie stared at the craft down in the bay. Anchored well out from the docks and surrounded by small sloops and smacks, the *Betty* looked like a whale among minnows. Growdy ignored the ship and Jamie as well: "Your men will be comin' to the inn—?"

"This evening," Mr. Pye said carelessly. "Say eight bells."

"Then they'll be wantin' supper," Growdy muttered.

"Aye," Mr. Pye agreed.

Growdy leaned close, and Jamie saw a quiver of distaste in Mr. Pye's expression. "Tell me," the innkeeper said in a confidential voice, "be ye pirates?"

Mr. Pye took his time in answering. "We are privateers," he said at last. "Captain Deadmon holds a private commission from His Majesty, King Carleton II, for operations against the Zamps, the Vrenkons, and other enemies of the Crown."

Mr. Growdy blinked at that. "Carleton the third, ye mean."

"I mean," Mr. Pye said, "Carleton the second, most gracious and sorcerous King of Anglavon and the North Country, bless his memory. Our captain's commission was granted fifty-one years ago. The present king has not seen fit to rescind it, and so by the law of the sea it remains in effect. Good day, sir."

Growdy stood scratching his bald spot as Pye clapped his hat on his head, gave a perfunctory bow, and strode away, the walking stick swinging briskly. "Fifty-one years indeed. The liar," he muttered. Turning, the portly innkeeper held out a thick-fingered hand. "Give it here."

Jamie sighed and put the clymento in Growdy's palm. "It was his gift to me."

Growdy swatted him hard on the head. "Gift indeed. Ye rogue! Do I feed ye for standin' about givin' backtalk? Inside and to work, ye worthless rascal." A kick added emphasis to the order, but Jamie had grown used to anticipating kicks from Mr. Growdy, and he evaded it easily.

"Well, Phineas," called the village physician, white-wigged Dr. Goodwin, from the table where he had just finished eating his luncheon, "was that man what I think he was?"

"A pirate," Growdy acknowledged. "One o' Captain Deadmon's men, says he—"

"What?" The quavering voice belonged to Mr. Finch, the most ancient man in the village. He got up from his seat at a nearby table and stood on shaking legs. "Deadmon, ye say?"

"Aye," Growdy acknowledged. "I never hear of 'im myself. Do the name mean aught to ye, grandsir Finch?"

The old man snorted. A blue vein throbbed beneath the thin skin of his forehead. "You're naught but a younker, Phineas Growdy. Do the name Deadmon mean aught, he asks. Why, man, Bloody Tradd was nothing to Octavius Deadmon; 'tis said that Grim Morgan hisself was feared o' the man. With my own eyes I seed Deadmon's flagship leadin' a squadron o' six frigates into battle, and the smallest o' them carried forty-four gun."

With a wink at Growdy, Dr. Goodwin asked, "And when was that, Mr. Finch?"

The old man scowled. Jamie, fetching some ale for two fishermen, paused to hear what Mr. Finch had to say: "Nay, I'm not daft from age. I recalls it well. 'Twas in the summer o' '90, when the Vrenkons was like to land on our very doorstep."

"And did you see this Captain Deadmon himself, pray?"

"Aye! A fine figger of a man, maybe thirty-five or six or along there, with broad shoulders and pride in his bearin'."

4

"Why, if the man was thirty-five then he'd be near eighty now," Growdy objected. "Ye must surely be mistook, grandsir Finch. Don't be angry, old man. Don't use your magic."

For a quivering minute Mr. Finch stood glaring at the other two. "I knows what I knows," he muttered at last, and leaving a scattering of coins to pay for his meal he stumped out.

"Touched," was Dr. Goodwin's opinion. "And he won't let me use my healing magic on him. These old folk think the healing art is quackery. So, Phineas, you say this pirate is coming to the inn this very night?"

"Aye, that's what he says. And he's bringin' a shipload of his scurvy mates to my inn this evening. Why do the rogues always pick my place, I'd like to know?"

"It's the signboard, sir," Jamie said, busying himself picking up the doctor's dirty dishes with a minimum of clatter. "If only you hadn't hired such an elderly artist to paint it—"

Growdy bellowed, "Impudence!" and drew back his hand for a blow, but the sound of rattling wheels and clattering hoofs from the roadway outside stopped him. "Here, ye rogue, there's the northbound coach in the courtyard. Go help the old lady and the princess stow their luggage aboard her, and that smartly. And then fetch my friend the doctor another pot of grog."

"Yes, sir." Jamie hurried to obey, and Squok made a sound a little like a preoccupied hen.

The boy found Mrs. Llewellen and the Princess Amelia waiting in the cobbled forecourt of the inn, their three boxes already stacked beside the door. "Here's the lad," Mrs. Llewellen said cheerfully. She was a bosomy gray-haired woman, neatly (though not expensively) dressed, and her charge, the princess Amelia, was a girl of fifteen, with auburn hair and chestnut brown eyes.

Neither of them, as far as Jamie could tell, possessed any magic, but they had been important guests for the past two days. Privately, Jamie thought that Amelia was conceited and proud, though everyone knew princesses were as common as mushrooms in the tiny crazy-quilt kingdoms of the West Country.

"Good-bye," Amelia said in a studied voice. "We have greatly

enjoyed our stay under your roof, and we bid you a royal farewell."
She sighed and turned to her governess. "There. Is that right?"

"Quite right, dearie," Mrs. Llewellen beamed. "Oh, won't your
mummy and da be proud of their little girl! All polished by foreign
travel and all."

"I don't *feel* polished," Amelia complained. She wore a pretty
red velvet traveling robe, but it was no richer than the sort of
clothing worn by any merchant's child. "And we only went as far
as Catterburgh, after all."

"There, there, child," sighed the governess. "We went as far
as five guldens could take us. I should think you'd be cheery to
be on your way home."

"Oh, I am. Though of course I'd really hoped to go to the land
of Faerie for my Grand Tour."

"Now, child," Mrs. Llewellen said fondly. "You know that these
days one must travel all the way to World's End to find a vessel
that goes there. I should feel quite giddy, standing on the very tip
of the world. And besides, passage on a faerie boat is so costly."

Amelia sounded apologetic: "I know, but our trip has been so
dull, Nanny. We never even saw any pirates."

Jamie had tied the boxes on the carrier behind the passenger
compartment of the coach. "That's about to change. We have some
pirates coming in tonight."

"Really?" Amelia's brown eyes went very round. "Oh, Nanny,
may we stay and see them?"

"No, dearie," Mrs. Llewellen said with indulgent affection.

"Don't blame you for wanting to see them, your highness,"
Jamie said with a smirk. "They're bloodthirsty as anything."

"Nanny?" Amelia said. "Please?"

Mrs. Llewellen gave Jamie a warning look. "No, dearie, we
simply can't. We've been gone nearly a month now. Your mummy
and da surely miss you."

Amelia sighed. "I suppose you're right. Only, when I saw the
name of the inn I thought there'd be lots of pirates here."

"I was just speaking to Mr. Growdy about that," Jamie said

with an air of importance. "It was a mistake, you see. You know the parrot in the great dining room?"

"Oh, yes," Amelia said. "But he wouldn't talk to us."

"Squok never talks. It's his way. Mr. Growdy bought him from a peddler not long after he opened the inn. It was just called 'The Inn' in those days, and Mr. Growdy thought that a better name would bring in more trade. So he hired a painter and told him to paint a sign naming the inn the Parrot's Roost, with a picture of Squok and all."

"Oh," said Amelia, nodding intelligently. But after a moment she heaved a great sigh. "I don't understand."

Jamie began to feel that knowing more than Amelia did was not much of a triumph after all. "Well, the painter was hard of hearing. He misunderstood what Mr. Growdy said and did a sign for the Pirate's Rest instead, and that's been the name of the place ever since." He leaned closer and confided, "Mr. Growdy hates it, but he's too stingy to have the sign painted over."

"I hope he doesn't," Amelia said with a glance up at the brightly painted signboard above the main door. "I like it."

"I do too," Jamie agreed. He paused to admire the sign, which showed a corpulent pirate reclining at his ease in a stout wooden chair, lifting a mug in a cheerful toast, his feet resting on the edge of a table. Better that, Jamie thought, than a picture of poor old molted Squok with the thin yellow patches in his feathers and the droopy, sad cast of his head.

The coachman came out, tooted three blasts on his horn, and cocked an eye at the princess and her governess. "Two for th' kingdom of Laurel, is it?"

"That is correct," said Mrs. Llewellen.

"Good-bye, potboy," said the princess. "And thank you ever so much for telling me the secret of the inn."

Jamie rolled his eyes. Girls! Even if they were princesses! But he managed to smile as he held the door open for them and saw them off. When the coach had rumbled away to the road and had turned east, heading for the highroad, he remembered that Mr.

Growdy had ordered him to freshen the doctor's grog. He hurried away, hoping he was not too late to avoid another thump on the head.

He was too late. The innkeeper, deep in conversation with Doctor Goodwin and one or two others, hardly glanced around as he slapped the back of Jamie's head with a hard palm. Jamie managed not to spill a drop as he slid the pewter pot before the physician.

"Aye," Mr. Growdy was saying. "If they stay too long, I'll have to have young Jamie there whistle 'em out of town, eh?" He winked at the doctor with exaggerated craftiness. "He can take care of 'em, I'll lay to that."

The doctor took a long pull at the grog. "Ahh," he said. "And what is this magical talent the lad has, Phineas? You've hinted about it often enough, but no one in the village seems to know just what it is."

Growdy glowered at Jamie. "Never ye mind, Doctor. Let's just say he does what I asks him. Get on, ye rogue! Stand all day a-gawpin' when work's to be done!"

Jamie went on his way, thoroughly hating Mr. Growdy, the inn, and everything connected with it. In his heart of hearts, he looked forward to the coming of the pirates.

They arrived that evening, Mr. Pye and seven others. Mr. Growdy met them with a great show of obsequiousness, bowing and smiling and promising all sorts of comforts that the inn did not actually afford. They were a taciturn lot, and somewhat disappointing to Jamie, for they were all quiet middle-aged men and not at all his idea of a cutthroat gang of bloody brigands. Worse, the captain of the vessel, Mr. Deadmon, did not come with them; Mr. Pye explained that the captain wished to remain aboard the ship to oversee the repairs.

"Action, was it?" Growdy asked.

Mr. Pye shrugged. "Some. We lost some yards and canvas in an exchange of fire with a Zampish frigate off New Clavall last winter. But it's mostly a case of wear and tear."

"Ah, to be sure. And you came here from a buccaneer's nest, no doubt?"

"From His Majesty's new world colony of Gloriana," Pye snapped. "Landlord, we are privateers, so belay your pirate talk, for we're not what you seem to wish us to be."

Growdy's face grew red. "Here, now. I wish nothing of the sort. I'm a loyal subject of the king—"

"To be sure. But now, landlord, we are hungry, so pray set us a table and let us eat."

Jamie's lot was to set the table and wait upon the guests. The eight of them hardly noticed Jamie as he bustled in and out, except to ask him for bread or more drink. But Jamie listened hard, with all his ears, as his mother used to say so long ago. He gathered that the eight were the officers and petty officers of the ship, and that the common sailors had found cheap lodgings down in the town.

Jamie felt honored to attend these men. Their talk of boardings and booty was music to him. Long before they had settled back with cheese and apples the boy found himself wishing fiercely that he could voyage with them over unknown seas and leave the sign of the Pirate's Rest behind him forever.

The sailors remained with them for five days, or rather for four nights, for it was their habit to rise at seven every morning, eat a hearty breakfast, and then amble down to the harbor to report to their captain. Jamie wondered what magic they had, for people with magical talents were about as common as left-handed people, and two of the officers were left-handed. He was disappointed, for none worked any wonders in his presence.

As often as not they were away all day, only to return at sunset with the appetites of wolves. "I should've told Pye room and board was two guldens," Growdy mourned, for with every meal the eight put beneath their belts he saw more of his profits vanishing.

Once or twice local folk, carpenters and victuallers, brought news of the ship. She had shot-holes to be patched, broken furniture to be mended, yardarms that had to be replaced, and she needed all sorts of foodstuffs. But though many of the local laboring magicians boarded the ship to do their work, they always dealt with Mr. Pye, and not one of them laid eyes on the mysterious captain of the vessel. Every night Mr. Pye and the other seven repaired to the inn after overseeing the work aboard ship.

The longer they stayed, the shorter Mr. Growdy's temper became. On the privateers' fifth night in the inn, as Jamie was busy cleaning the tables in the dining room, Mr. Growdy asked the first mate about the state of repairs aboard the *Betty*. "Nearly finished," Pye responded. It was a cool evening, and he stood with his back to a low fire in the common room's great stone fireplace.

"Ah and the victualling? Is it going well?"

Mr. Pye had taken out a long-stemmed clay pipe. For a few moments it seemed as if he would not answer as he used the fire tongs to apply a glowing ember to the tobacco and puffed the pipe to life. "Completed today," he said at last, turning to gaze down into the coals.

"Then I suppose ye'll be leavin' with a favorable wind?"

"We intend to sail at first opportunity."

"Ah, yes," said Growdy, rubbing his hands with his apron. "And, not meanin' to be inquisitive, ye understand, I wonder where your destination might be?"

Pye, looking more mournful than ever, shook his head. "That I do not know, innkeeper, for my captain's true destination we cannot reach. But I suppose we'll be for the Zampish Main again." He blew a smoke ring. It drifted toward the fireplace, where the draught caught it, and it vanished up the chimney. For two minutes or so Mr. Pye stood smoking in silence, while Mr. Growdy almost cringed at his elbow.

"They do say," Growdy put in at last with a sly wink, "that Captain Hawke and his crew be sailin' the waters hereabout."

Pye knocked the dottle from his pipe so sharply that he broke the stem. With a grunt he threw the broken pipe into the fire. "We'll not be joining the swine."

"But two ships sailing together, on account, as it were—"

Mr. Pye's sea blue eyes flashed. "Understand once and for all: We are *not* pirates. In our day, gentlemen of fortune were men of honor. Oh, what's the use? Good night, Mr. Growdy. I am in no mood for conversation."

The innkeeper sniffed. "Jamie," he said, "leave that. I'll want ye to come with me now, ye rascal."

Jamie felt his heart sink as he gave the table a few last wipes with a damp cloth. "Yes, sir."

Growdy grabbed his ear and tugged him along. The last glimpse Jamie had of Mr. Pye was of the tall man standing before the fireplace, long chin sunk on his breast, his arms crossed. He looked like a man hugging a secret sorrow close to his heart.

Growdy dragged Jamie painfully out the door and around to the side of the inn before he let go of the boy's ear. It was already full night; stars spangled the sky, and a cool breeze blew in from the water. "Now," Growdy said in a low voice, "whistle 'em out."

"Sir," Jamie pleaded. "You know magic hurts my head."

Growdy drew back a threatening hand. "I'll hurt your head for ye, ye whelp, if ye don't mind me in about half no time. They wants a fair wind. Whistle 'em up a good easterly."

Jamie quailed. "I'll be ill tomorrow," he warned.

"Nothin' so ill ye can't cure yourself by hard work, I warrant. Last chance, ye brat: Whistle up an east wind now!"

Jamie licked his lips. "I'll try," he said. "But I'm very tired."

"It don't have to be a gale, ye goose. Just such a wind as the captain will want to take advantage of. So it's best to make it a fair, moderate one. Do it, ye rogue."

For just a moment longer Jamie hesitated, for he thought he saw furtive movement from the corner of his eye. But when he looked, he saw only the yew trees that bordered the walk bending in the night wind. He wet his lips again, considered his repertoire, and then began softly to whistle the slow, sad old song of "East Wind Rising." As always, he had to think the words along with the music to get the tune just right:

Ho, the wind she quarters,
See, the sails do fill;
'Tis an east wind rising, lads,
To bring us naught but ill....

And before he had gotten through the first chorus, his head began to pound, as it always did when he whistled for wind. But the western gusts from the sea died away as the music flew between his pursed lips and out into the air. The restless yews stopped quivering and became still against the starry sky. Jamie continued the tune, and before long, an opposite wind, a light eastern breeze, began to stir. At first it was gentle, merely ruffling the very tops of the yews. Now Jamie whistled louder, coming to the mournful conclusion of the old sailors' lament:

See the east wind blowing
The foam from off the waves;
Tell our loved ones mourning
The seas shall be our graves!

"There," he gasped, holding his head in both hands. "Will that do, sir?"

Growdy sniffed the night air and involuntarily Jamie did the same. The reversed wind was bringing with it land smells: mown hay, cattle, the dryness of dust. The innkeeper grunted in satisfaction. "Aye, it'll do all right. Maybe with half a bit o' luck that pack o' thieves will leave with the tide in the mornin'. Get to bed with ye now, to sleep off that headache, for ye'll have a long day's work tomorrow a-cleanin' of them four rooms and all."

Jamie staggered around to the front of the inn, with Mr. Growdy slowly stumping after. The boy paused before the door; through the leaded glass panes he could see that Mr. Pye no longer stood in the common room. He glanced back over his shoulder and thought he saw the lanky form of the seaman striding down the road toward the harbor, but it might have been just headache or else the shadow of a cloud passing over the moon.

Mr. Growdy caught up and gave him a rough shove from be-hind. Jamie stumbled into the inn. Squok woke up and screeched, making Jamie groan, for his head was an agony now.

"Get to bed," Growdy ordered again. With no expectation of being able to sleep, Jamie crept to the cubbyhole near the kitchen where he spread his pallet. He slipped beneath the covers, fully dressed except for his shoes, and squeezed his eyes shut.

For a wonder, he fell asleep at once. And in the sleep a kindly dream visited him: He thought he was aboard a spanking sailing craft, riding easily before a gale, and that every moment the kindly wind swept him farther and farther away from Mr. Growdy and the sign of the Pirate's Rest.

CHAPTER 2

Kidnapped!

Jamie woke in darkness. That was no surprise, since his bedroom was only a disused pantry, but he sensed someone nearby, and in the dead of night that was unusual.

He sat up, groaning with headache. "Who's there?" he whispered, wishing he had a cat's magic talent of seeing in the dark. No answer came.

Tossing aside his blanket, Jamie groped out of the cubbyhole, the oak floor cold beneath his stockinged feet. Strong hands grabbed him, pinning his arms to his side, and another hand clapped over his mouth. "Got him," someone whispered. Someone seized his hands, he heard two finger snaps, and in a moment he felt the bite of rope magically tying itself to his wrists.

Jamie squirmed as he felt himself being bound hand and foot, but he could no more make a noise than he could fly. "Open hatches, matey," the whisperer said, and the hand was gone from his face. Jamie opened his mouth to yell. Too late: Someone tied a gag tightly in place. The cloth was rough against his tongue, though at least it tasted clean.

"Load cargo," the same man urged, "and cast off lines!"

Jamie felt himself hoisted onto someone's shoulder. One of the sailors, he supposed; certainly no one else in the village would want to kidnap him. His captors strode through the common room and out into the night. There they shifted him, with one person grasping the rope tying his hands, the other one binding his ankles. With his rear end hanging low, his arms and legs stretched high, Jamie felt the two men carry him along.

It was earliest morning, for in the west the moon had slipped low. Just past first quarter, it was too dim to allow Jamie to recognize his captors. The boy guessed that three or four of the privateers were jogging him along the cobbled road.

"Eh ee oh," he demanded as plainly as he could—not very plainly at all.

"What's that?" an unfamiliar voice snapped. Jamie did not recognize the speaker as one of the eight men who had put up at the inn. "What do ye want?" The man stooped, his breath warm and grog-scented in Jamie's face.

"Ae ee ah ow uh uh ow," the boy said.

The party halted near the arched wooden bridge that led into Gunnel Bay. The man said, "Can ye make him out, Sharkey?"

The man carrying Jamie's feet spoke in a low rumble: "Not I. Maybe ye should take the gag out, Cutler."

Jamie nodded vigorously. "Eh," he said. "Ae ee ah ow."

Cutler, evidently the leader, said, "I dunno. Mr. Pye's orders was to bring 'im gagged."

"Aye," Sharkey agreed. "But Mr. Pye didn't know he'd want to talk, I'll be bound."

"Ye may be right. P'rhaps I should let the lad speak."

Again Jamie nodded. Cutler leaned close. "Listen here, you," he said, his manner rough and menacing. "Ye're in the hands o' three desperate men—"

"Desperate? Oh, I don't know that's right, Mr. Cutler," interrupted a third voice, a rather mild one.

Cutler spun away from Jamie. "What, Wicks?"

Wicks, who held Jamie's bound hands, coughed delicately. "The desperate part, I mean."

Cutler snorted. "Oh? Ye think we're not desperate?"

Wicks shrugged, making Jamie swing to and fro. "Well, speakin' for myself, I'm not precisely desperate, no. Leastways, not near as desperate now as I was afore we had shore leave."

15

Sharkey asked, "Not desperate? How would ye describe your state o' mind?"

Wicks hesitated. "Well, I don't rightly know."

"Gloomy?" Cutler suggested.

"Gloomy? Nah, I wouldn't say that."

"Well," rumbled Sharkey, "are ye happy, then?"

Wicks laughed aloud. "Happy? Certainly not!"

"Pensive," said Cutler. "I'll wager ye're pensive."

"I expect not," Wicks said in thoughtful tones. "Mostly 'cause I don't know what it means."

"Come, come," scolded Cutler. "Ye must be *something*."

"Um ... enervated? Nah, that ain't it. Oh, I have it. I reckon I'm kind o' pessimistic, like."

"Right, then," said Cutler, and he stooped over Jamie again. "Lad, ye're in the hands o' two desperate men and one who's powerfully pessimistic at best. If I takes the gag out o' your mouth, will ye give me your solemn word as a kidnap victim not to call out?"

"I oo," said Jamie.

The men were silent for a long moment. "It's no good, is it?" asked Wicks sorrowfully. "He can't promise till ye take the gag out, and till he promises, ye can't ungag him."

"'Tis a hard knot for a sailor to unravel," observed Sharkey.

"Avast!" Cutler hissed. "The lad gave his promise."

"It won't do, Cutler," said Wicks. "We heard him, same as ye. 'Twasn't a understandable promise at all."

Sharkey grunted in agreement. "It ain't regular."

"Blazes!" Cutler retorted, though his voice was still only a loud whisper. "I never crossed the wake o' such seagoin' lawyers. Let me see. Boy, if ye'll give your affy-davy not to shout should we undo the gag, nod your head."

Jamie nodded.

"There. As ye've given your solemn promise—"

"He hasn't, you know," said Wicks.

Jamie heard Cutler take a deep breath. "As ye've given your solemn *nod,* I'll loosen the gag. But no tricks, mind! If ye dares to yell out, then we shall—we shall—"

"Drop you hard," said Sharkey with stern emphasis.

"And run away very fast," Wicks added helpfully.

"Lubbers," Cutler muttered with a snort. "Here." Jamie felt the knot give way and the gag slide out of his mouth.

Jamie licked his dry lips. "Thank you," he croaked. "Are you with Captain Deadmon's ship?"

"That we are," Cutler affirmed. "Fo'c'sle hands, and as stout a band of sea dogs as ever hoisted anchor."

"Then untie me and I'll walk. I want to join your crew."

"Thunder strike me," rumbled Sharkey.

"No, no," Cutler said at once. "It won't serve, lad. Orders we had to kidnap ye, and them orders we be a-carryin' out. Nary a word was spoke to us o' your joinin' the crew."

"P'rhaps we should ask Mr. Pye," said Wicks.

"Aye, Wicks. You run across the bridge and fetch Mr. Pye here. He'll know what to do." Wicks shifted Jamie again, doubling him over the broad shoulder of Sharkey.

"Can't I set him down?" rumbled Sharkey. "He's deuced heavy."

"Lad, will ye give me your word not to run away if we—"

"How can he run?" Sharkey asked. "He's all tied up."

Jamie heard a strange sound, something like the noise the cook at the inn made while grating nutmegs. It was the sound of Cutler grinding his teeth. "Will ye give me your word not to *hop* away if we put your feet on the deck?" he asked Jamie, biting off each word.

"I will."

"Lower away, lad," said Cutler. Grunting, Sharkey set the boy carefully upright. With his ankles bound, Jamie had some trouble keeping his balance, but he managed not to fall.

Now that he was standing, Jamie got his bearings. The bridge was not twenty feet away. Off to his right a light or two burned in the village. The inn, far off up the hill, was dark, for Growdy was as stingy about candles and lanterns as he was about anything. "Why are you kidnapping me?" Jamie asked.

"Don't know," Cutler confessed. He was a bulky silhouette, almost as short as Jamie. "The captain ordered us to, is all."

"We never questions orders," explained Sharkey. " 'Cept when we don't understand 'em."

"Which is most of the time, with you," Cutler retorted. "Belay the gabble." After a short silence, Jamie heard footsteps and the tap of a cane. He could barely make out that one of the two shadows crossing the bridge seemed to be wearing a tricornered hat. "What is the problem?" this person asked, his voice revealing him to be Mr. Pye.

"Please, sir," said Jamie, "I want to join your crew."

Mr. Pye stopped dead. "Join our—well, I'm dashed. Do you mean it, lad?"

"With all my heart, sir. I want to—to—"

Pye's voice was not unkind: "To get away from your master?"

"Well—yes, sir."

For a few seconds Mr. Pye tapped the ferrule of his cane against the cobbles. "Have you no family?"

"No, sir. My father died when I was three. My mother passed away four years ago."

The tapping ceased. "An orphan. How old are you, boy?"

"Almost sixteen, sir. I've never been to sea, but I have sailed in fishing boats. I can cook and clean, and I learn fast as anything. I'd be glad to work as cabin boy, or—"

Wicks interrupted: "Cabin boy? Please, Mr. Pye, take him, do. I would so like to be an able-bodied seaman at last."

Pye, sounding more indulgent than stern, said, "Hush, Wicks."

"But, sir, I was cabin boy when I joined the crew at fourteen. Now I'm thirty-four, and I'm still cabin boy. Nineteen blessed years o' the same thing, day in and day out, don't give a man much hope for advancement."

Ignoring him, Mr. Pye addressed Jamie: "This is a weighty decision, lad. You know nothing of our crew or of our captain."

"I don't care. The ship can't be worse than the inn."

"Knowing your master, I believe you." Mr. Pye tapped the cobbles again. "I cannot make this decision. It's for the captain to say. But consider this: We want you for one thing only. Should you prove able to help us in that one thing, then we'll set you free

18

as soon as it's done. Should you prove unable to help us, why, we'll set you free then too. *If* you're our captive, that is. But if you sign articles, you're a member of the crew. That means you can't leave the ship at a whim, nor will the captain release you from your pledge of service until our voyage is over. As you may have gathered from what Mr. Wicks said, that could be a very long time."

"I'll come willingly."

Somewhere a cock crowed, though the east showed no sign of dawn. "Untie him, then," Mr. Pye said at last.

Sharkey snapped his fingers once, and the ropes untied themselves from Jamie, crept like snakes to Sharkey, climbed his legs, and coiled themselves neatly around his shoulder. The boy stood rubbing his wrists and stamping his feet while his blood rushed back to toes and fingers with a pins-and-needles prickling. "Mr. Pye, might I ask one last favor?"

"You may ask."

"May I go back to get my shoes and one or two things? And to set Squok free?"

"Squok?" asked Sharkey.

"Our parrot," Jamie explained. "I feed him and give him water. Mr. Growdy'd be sure to forget."

Mr. Pye asked, "You're not planning to raise a hue and cry?"

"Oh, no, sir."

"On your honor?"

Jamie hesitated. Finally, he said, "I'm not quite sure what my honor is, sir. I don't even know if I have any."

"That's all right, then," said Sharkey in his rumbling voice. "For them as gives their word too quick is the ones as lack honor altogether."

Mr. Pye agreed: "My shipmate is right. Take it as given, lad, that you do have honor. Will you then swear on it to keep silence and return to us?"

"On my honor, sir."

"Run along and look sharp. We'll wait for you here."

"Yes, sir!"

"Say, 'Aye, aye, sir.' You might as well begin right."

Jamie stood up straight as a ramrod. "Aye, aye, sir!"

Running up the lane toward the inn, Jamie made good time despite his bare feet. He reached the door and found it was not locked—he had not expected it to be, since he had heard no sound of key or bolt when he was being carried out—and he tiptoed across the common room to his cubbyhole.

He found and lit a stub of candle. He tossed his spare shirt, breeches, and stockings onto a blanket. From a peg he took an ivory locket, which contained a miniature portrait of his mother as she had looked on her wedding day. He fastened the chain around his neck and slipped the locket inside his shirt. Finally he tied the four corners of the blanket together to make a sort of pouch, put his shoes on, and was ready to go.

He tiptoed very quietly across the common-room floor. Setting the candle on the table, he began to undo the cord that tied Squok's right leg to his perch. The bird woke and clacked his beak.

"Shh," Jamie whispered. "Time for you to get out of this, old fellow." He put his hand against Squok's chest. The parrot shuffled onto his fist, the claws pinching. Jamie slowly lowered his hand and Squok climbed sideways up to the boy's right shoulder. Jamie pinched out the candle, opened the door, and eased outside.

"Go on," Jamie said. "Fly away."

Squok did not budge. The bird's claws kneaded his shoulder. Possibly, Jamie thought, it was too dark for him to navigate.

"Oh, all right. Maybe the pirates will sign you on too. But it's likely to be a hard life for a bird." Jamie strode downhill. Now the moon, blurred by sea haze, was touching the horizon, and the eastern sky held streaks of gray.

At first he thought the sailors had deserted him, for they were nowhere in sight. But as he stepped onto the bridge, they melted out of the shadows. "Come on, then," said Mr. Pye. "Not a word until we're away from town!"

They crossed the deserted square. A gray cat paused to watch them pass, and Squok casually edged to Jamie's opposite shoulder.

Their footfalls raised soft echoes in the narrow streets, but not a soul challenged them. Though almost bursting with questions, Jamie dared not ask them for fear Mr. Pye would change his mind about kidnapping him. Trotting alongside the men in silence was one of the hardest things the boy had ever done.

The privateers turned eastward at the bay, away from the fishing craft tied at the piers. The tide was high, Jamie saw, but about to turn.

They came to a jolly boat hauled up on shore with three men standing beside it. Sharkey, Wicks, and Cutler helped them drag the boat down into the water. "Let's have your bag," Mr. Pye said, and he swung it into the stern. "And since you're a new hand, let me assist you as well." He boosted Jamie into the boat, climbed in himself, and then the six sailors pushed it away from shore and clambered aboard too.

In an instant the men had broken out the oars and fitted them; in another they had begun to pull, and the jolly boat shot across the water. "May I talk now?" Jamie asked.

Mr. Pye, away in the stern, had gripped the handle of a steering oar. Leaning comfortably back, he said, "Aye, lad."

Jamie cleared his throat. "I suppose the gentlemen who were staying in the inn are aboard ship now?"

For a moment Jamie thought Mr. Pye was not going to answer. But it was only the first mate's customary thoughtful pause; he rarely seemed to deliver himself of an unconsidered statement. Now he said, "Yes, for the captain called a council of war about you, and we all had to report aboard for that."

Jamie could not conceal his surprise. "About me, sir?"

"Aye, lad. When Mr. Growdy haled you away, I followed. I saw what you could do with the wind. That's a great gift, lad. Only about one person in ten is born with a magical talent, and most magic is not so useful."

"I know," Jamie muttered. "Lots of people in town can do useless magic. Old Mr. Finch changes wine into water, but that does nobody any good. One of the maids can make sheets fold themselves, sort of—they generally get tangled."

Sharkey snorted. "Landlubber magic," he said. "I can make ropes tie and untie themselves. We got a pilot—"

"Hush, Sharkey," Mr. Wicks said. "The boy is right. The lucky ones who are born with magic often find no use for the ability. It's a rare magician who can find a berth in life that suits his talent."

"I don't know that I'll ever find my berth," Jamie said. "My magic changes the wind, but it hurts my head something awful." The boy paused. "You were watching when I whistled. I saw you."

"Gettin' rusty in the skulkin' department, Mr. Pye," chided Cutler from the bow of the jolly boat.

Mr. Pye ignored the taunt. "I think your headaches are a thing of the past. Such pain comes of using your magic against your will. Only a wicked person can use his talent for wicked ends without a few touches of conscience—or headache. If you use magic wrongly, it always bites."

Ahead of them the three-masted craft suddenly materialized from the haze, a solid shape in the graying darkness. Cutler cried, "Ahoy, the *Betty!*"

Across the misty water came a reply in a voice Jamie knew from the inn: "Ahoy! Did ye fetch what was wanted?"

Mr. Pye sang out: "Aye, Mr. Tallow."

"Aboard with ye, then." Second mate Tallow's voice was as rusty as his red hair, a husky baritone that sometimes rattled like an anchor chain. "Captain Deadmon's not wantin' to waste the flood and the wind."

The jolly boat nudged the side of the larger vessel with a hollow thump. One of the sailors grabbed a line tossed down from the deck. Mr. Pye asked, "Can you climb a rope, Mr. Falconer?"

"Aye, aye," Jamie said.

"Then up with you. I'll bring your pack."

Squok was flustered by Jamie's scramble, but somehow or other the parrot kept his precarious grip on the boy's shoulder. Jamie went up hand over hand, the rope taut and hot in his grip. He used his feet to steady himself against the hull and found the going easier. Mr. Tallow gave him a strong hand up. "Well, well, come under your own power, matey?"

"Aye, aye," Jamie panted.

Tallow laughed. "A salt, by gar!"

The others climbed up, and last of all Jamie heard three finger snaps. Obediently the rope hauled itself aboard, bringing Mr. Sharkey with it. He joined the others in pulling away at lines, and in a moment the sailors brought the jolly boat aboard and lashed it down.

From the bow came the sharp rise and fall of a bo'sun's whistle, and suddenly men were everywhere, leaping into the rigging, fitting capstan bars, crying out in the strange language of the sea.

Mr. Pye put his hand on Jamie's unparroted shoulder. "Now, lad, we must get underway. It's late, and we've broken your sleep. I'd take it as a kindness if you'd turn in while we're lifting anchor and raising sail. I mean no offense, but you are a green hand, and likely to get underfoot."

"I'll try sir. But I'm too excited to sleep."

"Come with me."

Mr. Pye led him aft, through a narrow passage beneath the quarterdeck, lit with the soft glow of oil lamps mounted in gimbals. "Here," he said, sliding a panel. "This has been Mr. Wicks's berth for nigh twenty years, but if he's to become an A.B., he'll be moving to the forecastle before long. See if you can make do."

"It's fine," Jamie said, slipping into a narrow cabin barely large enough to contain a bunk. They had passed a lashed cannon, its muzzle close to a closed gun port, and Jamie had glimpsed another just past the sleeping compartment. With a sixteen-pounder not three feet from his head and another near his toes, Jamie felt that the enclosure was as grand as a palace.

As the boy climbed onto the bunk, Squok fluttered off his shoulder and perched on a narrow shelf on the bulkhead two feet above the pillow. "Ah. We have two new shipmates, not one," Mr. Pye observed, swinging Jamie's bundle of clothing onto the bunk. "I've work to do, so stay put until you're sent for. When we're underway, the captain will want a word with you. You just may change your mind and decide to be a prisoner."

"No fear of that."

"That's as may be. Now try to get a bit of sleep."

"Yes, Mr. Pye," said Jamie, who had just discovered a small porthole that gave him a glimpse of the village, the hill, and the distant inn, all standing out against the reddening sky.

Behind Jamie, Mr. Pye slid the panel closed. In a few seconds Jamie heard the rattle of anchor chains and the pattering of many callused bare feet as the sailors sprang to their duties. Lines creaked as the ship seemed to stretch like a cat waking from a nap. And then the village began to slide away. Despite himself, Jamie craned his neck to keep the inn on the hilltop in sight as long as he could. His father had been a sea captain, Jamie knew, but casting his memory back as far as he could, he could scarcely recall anything more than a hearty giant with a kind laugh and huge hands. Mr. Falconer had been lost at sea when his ship, the *Dolphin,* had gone down in a terrible storm.

His mother, left a young widow and lacking any magic of her own, had to make her own way in the world then. Because she had a good head for figures and could keep a book of accounts, she worked for Mr. Growdy. The Pirate's Rest had been Jamie's only home from his sixth year to that very night. Though it had been dismal enough after his mother died of a fever, still the place was familiar and known, and the sea was broad and mysterious. Now the old inn slipped out of sight astern of the *Betty.*

Jamie's heart thumped. No, the inn had not slipped away. It was the ship that was moving.

"Squok," he said aloud, "we're heading to sea!"

"Do tell," Squok observed dryly. "I'm overjoyed. Now, if you don't mind, I've got sleeping to do. I should like a bit of sea biscuit for breakfast."

Jamie started in surprise. "You talked!" he yelped.

The parrot cocked its beady eye at him, scratched itself beneath its beak, and yawned. It gave a sleepy muttered croak, ruffled its feathers, and closed its eyes.

Just enough gray light came through the porthole for Jamie to see that the bird was shamming. Its eyes were open the merest fraction, the black pupils gleaming.

"Talk again, please," Jamie coaxed.

The bird shuffled back and forth on the shelf, its tail rasping against the bulkhead. Huddling its head down into its shoulders, it pretended to snore.

"Oh, Squok, please," Jamie said.

But the parrot merely added a faint unconvincing whistle to the snore.

"Maybe I just dreamed you were talking," Jamie said. It suddenly came to him that the cabin boy's tiny berth was almost the same size as his sleeping compartment back in the inn.

"That's it," he told himself. "I'm probably back in the inn, after all. I fell asleep and dreamed I was kidnapped, and when I wake up it'll be because Mr. Growdy is pinching my ear, just the same as every morning." He felt decidedly let down.

But Jamie decided to make the best of his dream. He kicked off his shoes, stretched out on the bunk with his hands behind his head, and closed his eyes. It occurred to him that, if this were truly a dream, his head would not ache so much. But when he thought about it, he discovered that his headache was in fact a great deal better. He sighed in disappointment.

Presently the motion of the ship grew more pronounced, and Jamie supposed that he had dreamed the vessel out beyond the breakwater and into the open sea. He almost opened his eyes to look out the port, but he had grown very drowsy by that time. Before long he was dreaming for the second time that night—or was it the third? At any rate, he found himself lost in wonderful fantasies of cannonades and cutlasses, shouts and cries, mysterious islands and mountains of sparkling pirate treasure.

CHAPTER 3

Aboard the Privateer *Betty*

"Ouch!" Jamie writhed as someone pinched his right ear. "I'm awake, Mr. Growdy! I'm awake!"

He opened his eyes and saw not Mr. Growdy's cross countenance, but a bundle of green and red feathers. "Squok!"

The bird released his ear and bobbed its head. "Awk!" It hopped off his shoulder and back to the narrow shelf.

"Don't ever wake me that way." Rubbing his ear, Jamie swung his feet off the bunk and sat blinking. Morning light streamed through the round porthole. The bunk rolled with the motion of the ship.

"It's real," Jamie said, hardly daring to believe it. "I'm not in the Pirate's Rest. I'm really aboard a ship." He tumbled out of the bunk, reached for his shoes, thought better of it, and took off his stockings instead. Barefoot, he slid aside the panel and stepped into the narrow passage.

The rolling of the ship made it difficult for Jamie to walk, and he put a hand out to steady himself. From the berth behind him Squok fluttered up and landed on his shoulder. Jamie whispered, "Hungry? I don't have any crackers, but maybe we can find something."

The passageway was dim. The oil lamps had been extinguished, and only a little light filtered in from near the stern and around the edges of the closed gunports. Looking astern, Jamie saw another sliding panel, no doubt leading to a berth similar to his own, and across from that a regular doorway. The passage ended at a second door, probably leading to the stern cabins, and in this one a fan-shaped window glowed with daylight.

Instead of exploring that direction, Jamie turned away and started forward, trying to adjust to the ship's motion. He looked to his left and saw a ladder leading up to a grated hatch. Through the openings he glimpsed blue sky and dun-white sailcloth. Jamie continued forward, opened the door, and stepped out into the brilliant sunshine of a warm summer's morning.

Blinking, Jamie took a deep breath of salty air, then shaded his eyes and looked up. The mainmast seemed to tower all the way to the cloudless sky, and the square-rigged sails bellied out in a fresh wind—his wind, he thought with considerable pride. High atop the mast in the crow's nest, a lookout leaned easily on the rail. At that moment Jamie would have given anything to be up there, king of the sea, surveying his watery domain.

"Well," someone said. "I was told ye were not to stir until called for. Ye'll not advance far aboard this ship if ye don't follow orders."

Jamie jerked his gaze down from the heights. A skinny fellow of thirty-five with hair sun-bleached almost white stood grinning at him. Jamie blushed in embarrassment.

The sailor hastened to reassure him: "Well, 'tis time for ye to be about. No harm done, I'd say." There was something very familiar about the voice.

"Mr. Wicks?" Jamie asked.

"Aye, Davy Wicks, cabin boy of the good ship *Bouncing Betty Bowers*. But not for much longer, I hope—ye know what I mean." He winked a pearl gray eye.

"Oh. I—I hope so too."

Wicks looked around furtively, but all the sailors on deck were busy and none paid the slightest attention to the two. "Look here, lad, ye weren't joshing about wantin' to be cabin boy? My poor heart would break should ye have spoken false."

"No, I'll be cabin boy, if the captain will have me—" Jamie broke off. "Excuse me. What did you call the ship?"

"The *Bouncing Betty Bowers* she be called." Wicks looked the ship over, his chest swelling. "Right trim craft, ain't she?"

Squok shuffled restlessly on Jamie's right shoulder. Jamie reached up to ruffle the soft green feathers on the bird's breast. "Oh, yes, she's—Uh, Mr. Wicks, excuse me, but isn't that an—well, an odd sort of name for a privateer?"

Wicks shrugged. "It may be, but that's the name of this vessel. A sounder built craft never came out o' the yards. Cap'n Deadmon himself took her single-handed back when Pretender Jemmy tried his bit o' mischief."

"So long ago?" Jamie looked wonderingly about him, for the ship seemed much less than forty-seven years old, with fresh paint everywhere and everything in excellent order.

Mr. Wicks laughed. "I know, 'tis hard to believe. But I can tell ye this for certain: Ever since I joined the Cap'n, some twenty year ago, this here's been his ship, and he's kept her in tip-top repair."

"But—the *Bouncing Betty Bowers*?" Jamie said. "That seems such a silly name."

"Well, names is as names does, they do say. That's what she were called when she were took, and that's what she answers to today. And a good thing too, says I. 'Tis rotten bad luck to change the name o' a vessel."

The parrot puffed itself up and shook its feathers with a sound like a duster being wielded. Jamie pondered the notion of names and bad luck. "I never heard that."

"Oh, changin' the name of a vessel's the worst thing a crew can do, and ye may lay to that." Wicks's smiling face grew serious. "And whatever ye think o' the *Betty*, her name ain't never yet been disgraced by deed or word o' th' crew. Now ye'll be wantin' to see Mr. Pye to get your articles drawed up, or first maybe ye'll want a bite to eat?"

"Wrawk!" commented Squok.

"Uh—yes," Jamie said. "And I think the parrot would like some sea biscuit."

28

Mr. Wicks grinned. "We'll accommodate ye both." He reached out a forefinger and tickled the parrot's green breast. "Seems like old times, havin' a bird aboard. I recalls talk o' one sich bird that— ah, but ye're hungry. Stand agin the bulwark here, out o' sight, and I'll go ask Mr. Pye's permission t' wake ye. Be back in two shakes."

Jamie watched Mr. Wicks go up the curving stair against the starboard bulwark. He gazed out at the land, a purplish haze on the horizon. It gave Jamie an odd feeling to think that somewhere on that blur stood the Pirate's Rest and all the houses, churches, and shops that he had known.

But he had not much time for musing, for Mr. Wicks returned almost at once and accompanied Jamie up to the poop deck. Mr. Pye and Mr. Border, the bearded quartermaster whom Jamie remembered from the inn, stood close together near the rail.

"Here's the runagate," said stout Mr. Border with twinkling cheer. He wore his dark blue greatcoat and tricornered hat, the same costume Jamie had seen him in at the Pirate's Rest, but Mr. Pye had discarded his finery and looked rather dashing in black breeches, white hose, black silver-buckled shoes, and a voluminous white shirt tied at the waist with a red sash. "Well, lad," Border continued as Jamie came closer, "are you shipshape?"

Jamie remembered that the quartermaster was also the surgeon. "Quite well, thank you, sir."

"Excellent! Have you a stomach for breakfast?"

Jamie could not help grinning, for Border's good humor was infectious. "Aye, sir."

"Wicks, see to it, if you please," Mr. Pye said. "Let the boy dine in the wardroom. You may as well set out a bite for me too." Wicks hurried below.

Border chuckled and patted Jamie on the shoulder. "By the Powers, boy, I'm glad you don't suffer from *mal de mer*. There's nothing so disconcerting as a seasick prisoner."

With a quizzical smile, Mr. Pye said, "We have yet to settle on Mr. Falconer's status. Is he a prisoner or a recruit? What have you decided, lad?"

"Please, sir, I'd be happy to join the crew as cabin boy. Or anything."

Mr. Pye glanced at Mr. Border. "The lad has spirit."

"And who questions that?" Border said with bluff heartiness. "Not I, for I saw right off that he was made of sound stuff and that the rogue of an innkeeper was leading him a dog's life. What says the captain?"

Jamie's heart leaped to his throat. But Mr. Pye took his usual moment of deliberation before replying: "Captain Deadmon wishes to speak to Mr. Falconer first. He feels the lad deserves to know the whole state of affairs."

"Fair enough," said Border. "But, by the Powers, I admire the boy's pluck. If it's a close reach, tell the captain that Mr. Falconer has my backing."

"Thank you, sir," said Jamie.

Mr. Pye nodded in his melancholy way. "I suppose it's best to deal with these matters while we've a calm sea and a fair wind. Mr. Border, be so good as to notify Captain Deadmon that Mr. Falconer will wait upon him as soon as he's eaten breakfast."

"Aye," Border said, and with a cheerful wink he turned, raised a hatch, and climbed down the ladder.

"Steady as she goes, Mr. Yeoville," said Mr. Pye.

The helmsman, a barefoot old salt, responded, "Aye, aye, sir."

"Ship's wheels are a wonderful invention," Mr. Pye said in an offhand, musing sort of way. "One could write a poem about a ship's wheel."

Jamie was taken rather at a loss by this. "Indeed, Mr. Pye?"

The helmsman shook his head at Mr. Pye's philosophizing. "Shall I give the lad a sample o' steerin', sir?" asked Yeoville. "More useful knowledge than poetry and such like, if ye don't mind my sayin'."

Mr. Pye heaved a great sigh. "Jamie?"

But the boy had already sprung forward. Yeoville showed him how to grasp the wheel, how to stand with his feet apart and his legs braced, and cautioned him not to let the ship fall off from the wind. Then he took his hands away and Jamie was steering.

For a few seconds it was glorious. The ship felt like a spirited horse, trembling in its eagerness. But when Jamie tried experimentally to move the wheel just a little from side to side, it spun hard to port, and Yeoville stepped back into place with a chuckle. "Ye'll get the hang of it," he said. "Not bad for your first turn at the wheel."

Jamie felt his face burning with shame. Not bad was not nearly good enough.

Fortunately for Jamie's self-respect, at that instant Davy Wicks came into view again. "Breakfast is ready, sir."

"Thank you, Mr. Wicks. We shall go below as soon as Mr. Border returns," Pye acknowledged.

In a few moments more the quartermaster came huffing back up the ladder, closed the hatch, and said, "All's ready, Pye."

"Then the boy and I will have a bite to eat if you will be so good as to mind the ship."

Border took a deep sniff of the fresh air. "Aye, that I will. It's a pleasure on such a rare day as this. Warm sunshine, a calm sea, and a fair wind make me young again."

Mr. Pye led the way down. He paused to look at the set of the sails, to grasp a line and tug it experimentally, to glance over the rail at the wake as if estimating their speed. Then Jamie followed him through the port passage toward the stern.

They entered a large cabin, running the width of the ship and divided only by a screen in the center. A table was already set here with two plates, a pitcher of water, bread, sliced ham, cheese, grapes, apples, and a round pasty something that had to be sea biscuit, for Squok perked up at the sight of it.

Jamie fell to with a hearty appetite. Mr. Pye ate more abstemiously, limiting himself to a small slice of dark brown bread, a bit of ham, and one small wedge of cheese. He finished quickly and toyed with a small handbell beside his plate, not ringing it, but just twirling its handle between his thumb and forefinger in an absentminded way.

Meanwhile Squok fluttered to the table, waddled to the biscuit, and attacked it with relish, standing on one foot and breaking off bits of the biscuit with the other. Jamie laughed to see how the bird gobbled his breakfast so greedily, and when the biscuit was gone, he gave Squok several grapes, which the parrot ate with more delicacy.

"You'd think your bird had been at sea before," Mr. Pye remarked.

"I hope it's all right that I brought him. Poor old Squok didn't want to leave me last night."

"Quite all right, lad. The captain is fond of parrots and has often had one aboard. Indeed, we used to have a mascot much like this bird, years ago. Have you finished?"

"Yes, I think so, thank you."

"Then we shall wait upon the captain." Mr. Pye added in a quieter voice, "Let me caution you: Do not be disturbed by his appearance."

Jamie felt a stirring of uneasiness. "Sir?"

"He can be, well, rather appalling to some. But he is a man of honor, and his misfortune makes him none the less an able commander." Mr. Pye rose and rang the handbell. At once Wicks came back. "Mr. Wicks," Pye said, "tell the captain we are ready to speak to him, and then you may clear the table."

"Aye, aye, sir. And mayhap for the last time, eh?"

"We will see, Mr. Wicks. Mr. Falconer, come with me."

They did not go far—just around to the other side of the screen. There the cabin had been made into a sort of office, with pigeonholes full of papers, shelves of leather-bound books, a neat small desk, and a few chairs. Mr. Wicks made short work of speaking to the captain, for almost at once there came from behind the clatter of dishes as he tidied up the wardroom.

Curious, Jamie looked around the starboard side of the great cabin: through the transom windows he could see the ship's wake trailing out behind. "Excuse me, sir," he said. "I thought this would be the captain's quarters."

"It was, once," Mr. Pye said, looking grave. "But he no longer needs the cabin, and being a practical man, he's had it refashioned into the officers' mess and the ship's library."

"But where does he sleep?"

"He doesn't, though he sometimes rests in a sail locker."

Before Jamie could digest this news, the door opened and a tall, muscular man came slowly in.

"Captain Deadmon! Captain Deadmon!" The voice was a shrill shriek in Jamie's ear, and it took him a second to realize that Squok had spoken. The parrot launched itself from his shoulder and flew straight to the newcomer.

"What's this?" The man's voice was so hollow and toneless it sent a shiver down Jamie's spine. "By the Powers! It's the old Admiral himself!"

CHAPTER 4

Captain Deadmon

Squok landed on the newcomer's shoulder. "Cap'n Deadmon!" the bird cried. "Cats tear my tailfeathers, but you're a grand sight!"

"Sadly altered," the captain said in his hollow voice. "It must be thirty years since I lost the *Corsair* off Crossbone Cay. I imagined you'd gone down with the ship."

The bird puffed himself up. "Small chance. I flew clear and looked for lifeboats, but missed 'em in the smoke. I tried for the island, flew nearly ten leagues, and lit on the taffrail of that cursed Zampian. The blackguard took me prisoner and then sold me to a wandering peddler."

Mr. Pye shook his head, and his pigtail swayed like a pendulum. "Bless me, it is Admiral Green. I never thought I'd see him again."

"Good day to you, Mr. Pye," the parrot returned saucily. "First mate? You've risen in the world. Still scribbling?"

"Here," Deadmon said quietly. "Belay that."

Jamie plucked Mr. Pye's sleeve. The first mate glanced round, coughed, and said, "Sir, I am overjoyed that our old shipmate has rejoined us, but we do have other business. This is Jamie Falconer."

The captain came forward with a stiff and stately step. As the light from the transom windows fell on him, Jamie could not help blinking. Deadmon stood more than six feet tall, with broad shoulders and powerful-looking upper arms. He wore no hat, and his grizzled hair was closely cropped. He had fierce eyebrows, a hawk's beak of a nose, and a square, clean-shaven chin. But he did not look well.

His skin was a ghastly gray, and his dark eyes were fixed and glassy. His face lacked expression. There was an uncanny stillness about him. He stood regarding Jamie with that unnerving stare. He took a deep breath. "So. You can magically whistle up the wind, eh, lad?"

Jamie swallowed. "Yes, sir."

The captain's chest moved as he took another breath. "We have few enough aboard who can do such useful magic. So, so, Mr. Pye says you've had enough of shore life and want to join our crew."

"More than anything, sir."

The captain's face did not change. "Sit down, lad. And you, Andrew."

"Thank you, sir," said Mr. Pye, and he and Jamie sat.

The captain remained standing, staring at nothing. "I understand you are an orphan."

"Yes, sir."

For a moment Deadmon was silent. Then he took another deep breath. Jamie realized that he breathed only when he was about to talk; otherwise his chest neither rose nor fell. "Well, you had better know our situation. We're a rather dangerous crew. Mr. Pye, if you please."

"Aye, sir." Mr. Pye turned to Jamie. "Here's the way of it, lad. Captain Deadmon has been on a treasure hunt—"

"Treasure?" Jamie could not help exclaiming.

Mr. Pye frowned. "Hear me out, Jamie. Seeking treasure's not the lark landsmen think it is. The captain has been on this hunt for many weary years."

Deadmon gave a quiet but piteous groan. "Sixty long years and more."

Jamie's head whirled. Despite his gray hair, the captain looked scarcely sixty. Could he have been seeking treasure from the cradle?

Mr. Pye said, "I must explain the nature of that treasure hunt. What do you know of dragons, Jamie?"

Jamie frowned. "Dragons? Well, they're big serpents, but with legs and wings. And they breathe fire and eat young ladies and are very fierce. Only—aren't they just stories, sir?"

The parrot laughed. "Listen to the boy," it croaked. "See the sort of people I've been among, Cap'n? They don't even educate their nestlings."

Mr. Pye continued just as if there had been no interruption: "Dragons are, or were, real, Jamie. You have the right idea: They are indeed fierce, dangerous, and acquisitive. Of all treasures there are none anywhere—not in any emperor's palace, not in any fleet of galleons—to match the hoards of really old dragons. And that fact began our long, long voyage."

The captain took a breath. "Aye. I grieve to confess it, but long ago I was no privateer but an outright pirate. By the age of twenty-four I was the most feared captain on the sea."

"True, Cap'n," the parrot said fondly. "You were the pirate's pirate."

"Well, that's all past now," Deadmon said. "But when I was four-and-twenty, I swore a great and horrid oath."

When Deadmon broke off, Mr. Pye took up the tale again: "The captain had just won a fabulous prize. His first mate (for this was long before my time) said to him, 'You'll never take richer plunder than this, sir.' And then Captain Deadmon—shall I, sir?"

Deadmon's chest expanded. "I'll tell it. I swore by the most binding forces, by sea and wind and other Powers, that I would never rest until I had taken the richest of all prizes: a dragon's hoard. And there came a great thunderclap from a clear sky, and the very deep trembled. I knew I'd done an awful thing, but no captain can call back an oath once it's spoken."

"And did you fulfill the oath, sir?" Jamie asked.

Deadmon groaned.

Softly, Mr. Pye said, "There are few dragons left in the world, Jamie. In all the years since that oath, Captain Deadmon has heard of only three. Two of the tales proved false—only a lame wyvern

in the one case, and nothing but a reticulated python in the other. No other dragons linger in the lands washed by the seas we know. Save perhaps one only."

"The dragon of Windrose Island," Deadmon whispered. "Years ago, we came by a chart showing one last dragon's lair on Windrose Island. But we cannot discover whether or not the chart is true, for no favorable winds ever blow there."

Jamie sat up straighter. "I see. You want me to whistle up a good wind so you can get to this island."

"Aye," Deadmon said.

"Why, certainly—"

But Pye held up his hand. "Take a clove hitch, lad. You haven't heard everything. Sir, shall I?"

"Yes," said Deadmon in a voice so filled with despair that it wrung Jamie's heart.

"After he had sworn the oath, Captain Deadmon was compelled by all the Powers to fulfill it. His quest became a plain necessity. For the rest of his career he has done nothing except seek a dragon to plunder. His service to the King, his privateering exploits, all have been means to an end."

"A weary time," the captain said.

Mr. Pye nodded. "Twenty years ago, the very worst happened. I was third mate then, and Captain Deadmon was in command of a dozen ships and nearly a thousand men. We were engaged in action against Lavaile, the Zampish pirate, and were outnumbered two to one. Grapeshot flew thick in the air and the wind was sickly with the smell of powder and blood."

"Sorry I missed it," the parrot said.

Deadmon observed, "The foes fought well. They killed me."

Jamie blinked. "Sir?"

Softly, Pye said, "The captain is not speaking metaphorically. We had gone to hand-to-hand fighting, cutlasses and flintlocks. The devil Lavaile raised a musket, and Captain Deadmon fell with a ball through his heart."

Jamie felt the hair at the back of his neck prickling.

Deadmon took one of his great breaths. "I lay there stark

dead, thinking to myself, well, Octavius, you never fulfilled that oath. But a misty spirit came to me, its eyes the color of a storm cloud." The captain's chin drooped. "That spirit and mine sat together on my carcass and had a bit of a jaw. 'Well, Cap'n Deadmon!' said the spirit. 'Now thou'lt think twice before swearing such an oath.' Naturally, I knew what oath the spirit spoke of, but I judged it prudent not to mention it.

" 'Who are you?' says I.

" 'A messenger from other realms,' the spirit replied. 'Thou knowest well my purpose.'

" 'Aye,' said I to the spirit. 'If you've come to impress me, here I am, a poor soul ready for your orders.' "

Deadmon broke off and shook his head stiffly. He took another breath and resumed, "I hoped the spirit would conduct me aloft, for I had tried to live a seamanly sort of life, though I feared we would head alow, for I *had* been a pirate in my time. But neither was to be.

"The spirit laughed at me instead. 'Aye, Captain, I have orders for thee, and they'll be none to thy liking,' it said. 'Thy oath is an uncommonly binding one. Dead or alive, thou must fulfill it. Here be thy sailing orders from now to doomsday: Until thou dost plunder a dragon's hoard, thy soul will be kept in irons in this dead body. Not until thy vow is fulfilled shall the Powers loose that soul and send it to its final reward.' "

Jamie shivered. "That's terrible."

Deadmon, who had required several breaths to tell his story, took another. "Aye, terrible. The spirit left me. My own spirit sat on my body, all struck dumb. Then it came to me that all the time the spirit had been talking, the fight had been raging. But it seemed dim and misty so long as my own spirit was on shore leave."

Mr. Pye added, "So far as we could tell, our captain lay dead on the deck. We had lost heart."

"Aye," Deadmon said. "They were in a bad way. Well, there my spirit sat on my own carcass, watching my men losing the fight. Then the desire rose in me to help my lads out. Before I knew it, I found myself back in my body, and my limbs moved to my will, though my heart had ceased to beat. I rose up, drew my cutlass, and led the men to victory."

"Good for you," said the parrot.

Mr. Pye smiled in his melancholy way. "Aye, Captain Deadmon gave Lavaile the fright of his life. All of us, foe and friend alike, froze when the two commanders closed. Captain Deadmon drove his foe to the rail, and the coward leaped over. When Lavaile sank, a great cheer went up on our side, we took heart and fought twice as hard, and we carried the day."

"And then most of my men deserted me," Deadmon said.

Pye nodded. "Captain Deadmon, out of a native delicacy of character, gathered us all together that evening and told us the whole truth. He gave us the opportunity of leaving him if we wished. Most of the crew did—including almost all of our magicians."

Deadmon said, "Didn't want to follow a living corpse. But bless their souls, some of my crew didn't mind."

"Nine hundred and eighty-odd men survived the battle," Mr. Pye said. "Of that number, just a hundred and twenty of us remained with the captain. We took this craft. The rest took our other ships or made off in the captured vessels. And for twenty years, Captain Deadmon has been a dead man, but still the captain of the *Betty*."

Deadmon heaved another great breath. "Aye. But though I pay no heed to time now—except I know it passes, and it seems more wearisome to me than when I was man alive—though time does not touch me, I say, it touches my poor crew. We lose men in sea-battles or just to age and illness. The *Betty*'s down to seventy-six men and fourteen guns."

"A sad state," Mr. Pye said, "when you recollect that a thousand men once leaped to Captain Deadmon's orders." The first mate leaned forward, his dark blue eyes intense. "Jamie, you say you want to sign on, but consider well. The *Betty* is not just any ship. Her fate is tied to her captain's. Her voyage shall not end until his does."

Jamie swallowed. "You mean that we may not be able to find the dragon on Windrose Island."

Pye sighed. "There may be no dragon. Or the dragon may prove too powerful for us. No one's fought a real dragon since the days of the Wizard-King Balmazor, seven hundred years ago."

For some moments there was silence in the cabin. Jamie finally broke it in a timid voice: "If we fail, there may never be another chance. Is that it, sir? And then I'll have to serve aboard the *Betty* for the rest of my life?"

Deadmon said, "Aye, lad. Maybe you'll be happier as our prisoner, not our shipmate. If all goes well, we'll set you free after our attempt on Windrose Island. At worst, you'd perish assaulting a dragon, but that would be true whether you were a crewman or a captive."

"Aye," said Mr. Pye. "And we are still a privateer crew. We take enemy ships when we may, and we do have our enemies. We might be attacked at any time by Vrenkon or Zampish ships—or by pirates."

"One in particular," said Captain Deadmon. "Hawke."

Mr. Pye's face darkened with disapproval. "A traitor to the Crown; an out-and-out pirate, with no respect for flag or loyalty. It's whispered that Hawke knows we have a chart to a dragon's treasure, and that he covets it. And Hawke commands more than twenty sail. If he encounters the *Betty* before we reach Windrose Island, we're in for a desperate fight. Hawke is an ambitious man and yearns to be known as the pirate who scuttled the famous Captain Deadmon."

"Our course lies between reefs and shallows," Captain Deadmon murmured. "And our numbers are few. We've had no new crewman since Mr. Wicks joined us, a few weeks before my fatal encounter. The fact is, no sailors care to join us nowadays."

Mr. Pye coughed. "The captain has too many scruples to impress an unwilling crew. So here are the sad remnant, a middle-aged lot. You'll find little to amuse a young fellow like yourself if you stay among us."

"There it is," Captain Deadmon finished. "Do you want time to decide?"

Looking at the captain, with his gray pallor and his glassy, vacant eyes, Jamie no longer felt afraid. "Sir," he said. "Excuse me. It's impertinence, I know, but—well, sir, how does it feel to be dead?"

Pye darted a surprised look at Jamie, but Deadmon simply took another of his bellowslike breaths. "Wearisome, lad. My soul knows it should have reported to its commander years ago, and it pines to find its eternal berth in that great fleet in the sky. On the other hand, there are advantages. I save a great deal of time, for I never have to breathe except to talk, and since I never sleep, I can ponder philosophical questions to my heart's content. It's thrifty too, for I don't eat. Dead men don't bite, you know."

"I meant no disrespect, sir," Jamie swallowed. "I need no time to consider. I am ready to sign aboard the *Betty.*"

"Hurrah!" cried the parrot. "Stout lad! Take him, Cap'n, do."

"Very well," Deadmon said. "Since you have decided of your own free will, so be it. Mr. Pye, draw up articles; Mr. Falconer is to join us as cabin boy and wind-raiser. You will promote Mr. Wicks to able-bodied seaman, and increase his share of the profits accordingly. Mr. Falconer, Mr. Wicks has been sailing these twenty years for a hundred and fiftieth part of the booty. Since you will have additional duties with the wind, let us say your share will be a hundred and twenty-fifth part. Is that amount agreeable to you?"

The parrot on Deadmon's shoulder nodded vigorously, so Jamie said, "Yes, sir," though he had not the least idea what such a share might mean.

"Mr. Pye will explain your duties. Admiral Green, would you object to Mr. Falconer's attending to your needs?"

"No, Cap'n," returned the bird. "I'll help train him."

"Good idea," Deadmon agreed. "Listen to Admiral Green, young Falconer, for he has spent much of his life at sea and has smelled powder more than once."

"Yes, sir," Jamie said doubtfully. "Only—I've always heard parrots don't know what they're saying. They only repeat what they've heard without understanding."

"Most parrots, perhaps," said Deadmon. "But this one is different. I suspect all of 'em may be, and they only pretend to stupidity out of arrogance and exasperation with the follies of mankind—eh, Admiral Green?"

"That would be telling, Cap'n," the parrot said.

"It's clear that Admiral Green knows what he's talking about, which is a good deal more than I can say for most sailors. Don't let his being a bird prejudice you, for he's a smart old fellow. I have it on good authority that parrots live forever, mostly, and experience is a great teacher."

"I'll listen to Squo—I mean to Admiral Green, sir."

"Good. Go to the boy, Admiral Green."

The parrot flew to resume its former perch.

"I shall leave you now. Mr. Pye will make all the necessary arrangements. Welcome aboard, Mr. Falconer."

"Stand up and salute," the parrot whispered.

Jamie did as the bird told him. "Thank you, sir. I shall try to be a good sailor."

Deadmon nodded, turned, and left the cabin. "Well," said Mr. Pye, "you made a favorable impression, Jamie."

"Thank you, sir."

"It will take some time to draw up your articles. If you like, you may tour the ship until they're ready." Mr. Pye gave one of his rare, melancholy smiles. "Make the best of your chance, for in days to come you may look back with regret on your last hours of freedom."

"Excuse me, sir, but—I have another impertinent question."

"Best ask it while you are still just Jamie Falconer and not Cabin boy Falconer."

"Is that what's wrong with you, sir? Do you regret being a member of Captain Deadmon's crew?"

Mr. Pye put his long hands together and rested his chin on the tips of his fingers. "No. I have served Captain Deadmon man and boy, alive and dead, for thirty-one years. Not once have I repented my decision to follow him."

"But you seem so—pardon me, sir—so sad."

Mr. Pye nodded. "Perhaps one day I shall tell you why. But my sorrow is an old one, going back to the time before I ever met

Captain Deadmon. Given the chance to leave him this minute, I would not take it. Is that satisfactory?"

"Yes," whispered the parrot.

"Aye, aye, sir," said Jamie.

Mr. Pye rose from his seat. "Along with you, now. I'll let you take the glad news to Mr. Wicks, and have him see me to rewrite his own articles. And you might help him move his sea bag to the forecastle, for he'll be joining the crew before the mast."

Jamie retraced his steps to the gun deck, where he found Wicks anxiously waiting. The former cabin boy cheered when he heard the news, and then he rushed to gather his possessions from his old berth.

Left alone, Jamie twisted his neck to look at the parrot. "Shall I call you Admiral Green, or Squok?"

The bird shrugged. "Either."

"Squok, then, for you're probably the only soul aboard that I won't have to say 'sir' to, and if I call you Admiral Green, I'll lose even that. You should have spoken to me long before this."

Squok sniffed. "For a seagoing parrot, no landsman's worth talking to."

"At least you're talking now." Jamie hesitated, and then asked the question that was plaguing him: "Did I do well, Squok?"

The bird considered. "Aye," it said at last. "Passably well. Only tomorrow see that the sea biscuit is crumbled before you serve it. And tonight I'd like a nice bit of fruit for supper. Not grapes, for too many of them upset my craw, but perhaps a nice apple or a good mellow pear."

"Ordered around by a parrot," Jamie said, but he could not keep from grinning.

Squok shrugged again. "You're a cabin boy now. You might as well get used to it."

CHAPTER 5

The Raid on Pridden Town

"Lessons!" Jamie grumbled. He tried again to memorize the Classic Vrenkish verb declension "azhbat, azhbath, azhbo."

He had not expected lessons when he signed his articles, but Mr. Pye insisted. "Lessons are traditional for a cabin boy. Mr. Wicks had them," Pye pointed out on the morning of the second day, when Jamie learned of his fate. "He can calculate accurately, read Vrenkish, and even quote the ancient wise man Skolastis when pressed. Perhaps it will seem easier if you regard being educated as part of your duties."

"But, sir," Jamie had objected. "I only want to be a sailor."

"You may not want to be a sailor all your life," Mr. Pye returned. "Why, you may wish to go to University eventually. You may have a vocation for business, or even for the law (indeed, many pirates have found the law an ideal second career), and so you must prepare."

"No sailor goes to University," Jamie argued. "You didn't, did you?"

Mr. Pye dropped his gaze and sighed deeply. "Indeed I did, lad. But no more of that."

In the end Jamie's protests were useless. Mr. Border, who lacked healing magic but really was a schooled physician and something of a naturalist, became his tutor in the natural sciences and the various branches of mathematics. Mr. Tallow undertook to teach him astronomy and navigation. And finally, Mr. Pye himself was Jamie's master for Vrenkish, elocution, composition, and literature. The only thing lacking was music, but with his whistling the boy already had a talent for that.

Jamie had to study, write, or recite four or five hours a day. It was almost more than he could bear—especially when the great cabin held so many artifacts that interested him more than books. There were a crocodile's skull, a fragment of a roc's egg, and a wicked Kratorian scimitar. Even better, a curious case covered in embroidered red and yellow silk enclosed two very small pistols with handles inlaid with silver filigree. Mr. Pye said that they had been made for an eastern potentate's young son, and he warned Jamie not to touch them, for they were not playthings.

And so Jamie was stuck with the lessons. In compensation, he was an actual member of the crew with regular duties. These he attended to with great diligence. He surprised himself, for his work was much like the tasks he had done back in the Pirate's Rest. He served meals to the officers, kept their cabins and the wardroom tidy, ran whatever errands were needed, and got underfoot at the most inconvenient times.

Strangely, though—and here was the surprise—what had been drudgery in the inn was delight aboard the *Betty*. He supposed it was simply that the ship was new and exciting. At any rate, he settled rapidly into the routine and made no more mistakes than he could bear.

For three days after their departure from Gunnel Bay the *Betty* beat up and down the coast as the sailors tried the new sails and became accustomed to the differences in handling the new rudder caused. Jamie reacquainted himself with all the officers and got to know many of the men. Most seemed to like and accept him, but he detected in them all a weariness brought on, he supposed, by their long years of service, with no end in sight.

Mr. Cutler, the boatswain, was typical. Though he was good at his job, his temper had been worn thin by years of repetitious routine. A strongly built man of forty-five, he seemed always busy, and in the rare intervals when he had nothing in particular to do, he was distant. Jamie's idea of worthwhile lessons was anything that would teach him more about ships, for he had only been aboard the tiniest of fishing boats before. He sought out other sailors to learn how to raise sail, how to climb the shrouds to the masts, how to do all the things that men before the mast had to do, but he never asked Cutler's advice. The boatswain was unapproachable.

It surprised Jamie, then, when one morning Cutler spoke up, apparently to him, to say in a wistful voice, "I'd give my good right arm to serve in a ship of the line again."

Jamie, who had been leaning over the forward rail to watch the wake cream away from the ship's prow, slipped down to the deck and said, "Sir?"

"Don't 'sir' me," Cutler muttered. "I'm no officer."

"Sorry, Mr. Cutler. I thought you spoke to me."

"Only to myself." Cutler sighed. "Ye know, Cap'n Deadmon was once in the Royal Navy. I served in a sloop of war in his fleet when I was no older than you. That were the life! Regular standing orders, a patch o' sea to patrol, and none of this blessed hustling from zone to zone in search of a blessed mythological beast. I can't complain o' bad treatment, nor would I speak against the Cap'n. But, by my hand, it would be so good to serve in a regular naval craft again."

A commotion in the ship's waist distracted Jamie. "I will, I tells ye!" shouted a deep phlegmy voice. "Blast ye to blazes and salt and pepper ye, I will!" A burly potbellied man, bald save for a laurel crown of curly white hair, shirtless and clad only in short breeches, lumbered up from the galley, wielding a large meat cleaver. Smoke-blackened and soot-stained he was, with glaring eyes and a nose as red as a spring pippin. In his wake danced an anxious group of four sailors, among whom Jamie recognized Wicks, all of them importuning the sooty man.

"Now, Timson," said Wicks, "ye don't have to. The boys are glad to give ye a bit of a rest—"

"Skillets and stewpots!" yelled the man called Timson. "Am I the sea-cook, or am I not?"

"Ye are," Wicks said in a placating way. "Ye are, Barbecue, and—"

"Then, by salt pork and sea biscuit, tonight I cooks!"

Mr. Cutler groaned. Jamie whispered to him, "Who is that?"

"Tim Timson, lad," Cutler returned in an equally low voice. "The boys call him 'Barbecue.' He's the *Betty*'s cook."

"What say ye to this?" Timson, hard by the port rail, roared to his entourage. "Codfish steak with seaweed sauce? Clam chowder? Sea cucumber salad? Don't your mouths fairly water, boys? Yum, I says by the devil's cookstove; and yum again, says I!"

"But, Barbecue," one of the other sailors cried, "the last time you made chowder you left the clamshells in."

Timson shook his cleaver alarmingly in the man's face. "Hard grub makes hard sailors, ye lubber. And didn't ye eat it?"

The man gulped audibly. "Of course, Barbecue, but—"

Timson turned on his heel and, still ranting, stalked off astern, the others following him and begging. "What's wrong?" Jamie asked Cutler.

The boatswain shook his head. "Every once in awhile Barbecue gets the urge to cook. Usual, he leaves it to his mates, and then things is all right, but once or twice a month he asserts his privilege, as they say, and then it's foul weather." He shivered and lowered his voice: "They say Cap'n Deadmon is the only man the pirate Tradd was feared of, but afore he died, Deadmon hisself was afeared o' Barbecue."

"Why?" Jamie asked, feeling shivery.

"Faith, lad, he's the worst cook as ever sailed the seas," Cutler whispered. "Cross him, and it's nothing but fish-head soup for weeks. And, ugh, such soup!" Cutler gagged.

"Why doesn't the captain name a new cook?"

The boatswain shook his head sadly. "When Barbecue signed his articles, he said he wanted to be a ship's cook. Thinkin' he'd learn his craft, Deadmon agreed. Well, here he is years and years later, and no better a cook now than he were at the beginning. Turns out he has a magic talent of makin' flavors more intense, which would be all right if the flavors was palatable to begin with. But when they're such flavors as a bad cook produces—ugh! Yet Timson signed his blasted articles, and still he wants nothing more than to be a sea-cook. And so cook he stays, for as Deadmon says, a promise is a promise."

At the time Jamie thought Cutler's fears were exaggerated, but that night, after choking down a generous serving of codfish steak dripping with a glutinous green mess (seaweed sauce, he presumed), he was of the boatswain's opinion.

The next morning he still had a stomachache as he sat in the stern cabin trying to decline the tedious Vrenkish verbs. It was hard going, and Jamie felt relief when Squok fluttered in and landed with very little grace on his head. "On deck," the parrot squawked.

"Ouch!" Jamie said. "Thanks for interrupting my lessons, but your claws are awfully sharp. At least get on my shoulder."

Squok hopped to Jamie's left shoulder and burped. "I feel sick," the bird announced.

"You ate the codfish last night," Jamie said.

"Aye. Do I look green?"

Jamie pulled his head back to squint at him. "Squok, you always look green."

"Aye," said the parrot, brightening. "I'd forgotten that."

Jamie found Mr. Pye and Captain Deadmon both on deck. "Here he is," Pye said. "Jamie, we're ready for a month-long haul to Windrose Island. But you're under-equipped for the voyage."

"Sir?" Jamie asked.

"You have but two suits of clothing," Deadmon pointed out, "and only one pair of stockings and shoes. We need to provide for you better than that, for we'll be at sea many long weeks before we'll have the opportunity again."

"Thank you, sir," Jamie said. "But I really don't need anything more."

"Tush," Pye said. "It's all settled."

"Aye," Deadmon said in his hollow voice. The captain was a

more unsettling sight in the light of day than in the dimness of the cabin, for his glassy stare was unnatural when he did not squint or blink even with the sun in his face.

"I have no money," Jamie said in a small voice.

Mr. Pye gave one of his rare, melancholy smiles. "How is this?" He held out a leather purse, somehow familiar.

Jamie gasped. "Mr. Growdy's moneybag!"

"Aye. Mr. Wicks sneaked into his room and relieved him of it the night you were kidnapped."

"They stole Mr. Growdy's money?" Jamie exclaimed, imagining the innkeeper's apoplectic reaction to such an act.

"Well," Pye said with a roguish smile, "he *did* want us to be pirates. Now, we're close to Pridden Town. We'll lay off the coast, and you and I will take the pinnace in to the harbor for supplies. Be ready by three bells, and you can steer the pinnace."

"Aye, aye," Jamie said smartly, for steering made all the difference.

Jamie was conscientious about his studies that morning, and not too long past noon, when he came on deck again, the ship had drawn close to shore. They stood off from the mainland in the lee of a cluster of rocky offshore islands, since the captain did not plan to enter the harbor.

Jamie put on his best shirt and the breeches that had only one small hole in the left knee. For the first day since he had come aboard, he wore his old shoes, down at heels and scuffed to bare leather. Mr. Pye too donned his shore clothes, the maroon greatcoat, tricorn, cane, and sword.

The sailors broke out the pinnace, a sailboat much larger than the jolly boat, and Mr. Pye, Wicks, and huge, lumbering Ned Sharkey accompanied Jamie down into the craft. Sharkey snapped his fingers and the lines ran up the single triangular sail. Feeling most important, Jamie sat in the stern of the craft, the tiller snug under his right arm.

The spell Jamie had cast on the wind had long since worn off, and this afternoon the breeze had shifted around to a good, steady blow from the south-southwest. Leaning against it, the pinnace skimmed across the water and into the harbor. It was a delight to feel the pinnace's responsiveness on the glassy, calm water. She glided with the grace of a swan and none of the pitching and bobbing of an ordinary boat, Jamie thought.

"Town's deuced quiet," rumbled Sharkey when they had drawn so close that Jamie could read the signs of the waterfront shops. "'Tain't the Sabbath, is it?"

"No," Wicks replied. "That's day after t'morrow."

"Stand by to luff," Mr. Pye ordered.

The two sailors and Jamie handled the pinnace so neatly that it slipped right into position beside a wharf. With a few snaps of Sharkey's fingers, the bow line snaked up to a piling and made itself fast. Wicks gave Jamie a good-natured hand up, and the four sailors walked down the dock, across a cobbled street, and into Pridden Town.

The half-timbered buildings reminded Jamie of Gunnel Bay. As in his hometown, Pridden's waterfront street was given over to lading houses, warehouses, grog shops, and other maritime enterprises, but Pridden was shut up tight. Boards covered many of the windows, and the doors were locked. No one responded to the sailors' pounding.

"There's some mischief about," observed Wicks.

"Aye," Mr. Pye responded. "What could have happened?"

They took a narrow street leading away from the docks and soon were in the heart of the little town. Still they found all the shops locked, all the houses deserted, though Sharkey said that he noticed a curtain twitch briefly aside in the window over one shop.

Pye said at last, "Lads, it's clear they don't wish our custom. I suppose we'd best return—"

"Get 'em!" The cry came from behind, and Jamie whirled. A half-dozen men, five of them big bruisers armed with handspikes and clubs, rushed the party. Mr. Pye put his left hand on Jamie's chest and pushed him; as the boy staggered back, he saw the first mate draw his saber and the other two sailors produce their gullies, brandishing the knives at their attackers.

The heel of his worn left shoe came loose and tripped him, and Jamie sat down hard on the cobbled street. He had a confused glimpse of Mr. Pye swinging his sword in a whistling arc, heard the splintering of wood as his blade caught a staff wielded by one of the six attackers, and at the same time one of the strangers leaped at him, raising a handspike high to strike.

Jamie rolled, kicking off his other shoe. A hogshead barrel stood against the front of the nearest shop, and Jamie fetched up against it with a jolt that knocked the breath from his lungs. The attacker brought his weapon down hard. Jamie flinched away and in the same instant the man yelped in pain as the spike slammed against the rim of the barrel. Jamie kicked the man on the shin, but his bare foot did no real damage.

A split second later Wicks brought the hilt of his knife down on the fellow's skull. Jamie winced at the hollow thud. The man's legs went loose, and he toppled forward onto his face at Jamie's feet. Jamie retrieved the handspike the man had dropped and sprang up to join the fray.

He was too late. Two of the attackers had taken to their heels. Two others lay unconscious, and the last two sat holding bruised heads and groaning. Mr. Pye stooped, grasped the collar of one of these, and hauled the fellow to his feet as easily as though he were a straw-stuffed puppet. "Now," he said, giving the man a shake, "perhaps you'll explain why Pridden Town gives visitors such a rude welcome."

The man spat at Pye's feet. "Cursed pirates. Not enough you robbed us yesterday, is it, then? You had to come back. What d'you plan to do today, then? Burn down our houses around our ears, is it?"

Mr. Pye shook him again. "You're mistaken. We've come to do business with some of your shops, that's all."

The other strangers were stirring and groaning. The man in Pye's grip said, "Jinks, I thought you recognized these vagabonds as members of the crew that sacked us yesterday!"

"Faith," moaned a hefty fellow guarded by Wicks, "they wore sea clothing, didn't they?"

Chagrin showed on the bruised visage of the man in Pye's grip. "I don't suppose you stopped to think that we're a harbor town, did you? That most of our visitors wear seaman's clothes?"

"Come, Marphy," said the fourth man, the shortest and slightest of the four, staggering to his feet. "You can't blame Jinks for being jumpy."

Marphy, who seemed to have some authority among them, shook his head and growled, "Warder Lovis, I think we may safely release these fellows from custody."

"If you say so, Mayor Marphy," said Pye's captive. "All right, then. You may go. But let this be a warning to you."

Though he rolled his eyes heavenward, Pye replaced his sword in its scabbard and turned to the mayor, a thin, short man with wild dark hair and a bruised cheek. "Sir, do I understand that pirates lately raided this town?"

"They did," said Marphy. "Yesterday the rascals rampaged through our streets, smashing windows, grabbing everything loose."

"What ship?"

The mayor looked at the warder. "Lovis, you saw the ship. What was she called?"

"The *Flying Terror*. A sloop, painted black with yellow trim."

Jamie had picked up his shoes and had come to stand beside Pye. He heard the first mate draw in a sharp breath. "Hawke's men," Mr. Pye said. "Wicks, Sharkey, put away your knives. The captain will want this news."

"Here," said the mayor. "I thought you wanted to trade with our merchants."

"Quickly," Pye said. "Where's the best shop to buy clothing and shoes for the boy?"

"Mine, of course," said the mayor brightly.

The mayor's place proved to be a well-stocked establishment far enough from the harbor to have escaped Hawke's ruffians. Though Mr. Pye was in a great hurry, he did insist on Jamie's getting a good stock of clothing: two pairs of shoes, better made than any he had ever owned, along with several sets of underwear and pairs of stockings, six pairs of breeches (one of them natty blue, for shore wear), six shirts, some colorful kerchiefs, a wool jacket, and a foul-weather cloak.

Sharkey took the bundle and swung it along as they made their way back to the harbor. The town had come alive now, and men and women stood sweeping the pavement before their shops, chatting, and giving the sailors suspicious looks.

"Didn't know Hawke was this close," Sharkey said as they turned toward the wharves.

"Nor did anyone," Pye said.

"Why is Captain Hawke after us?" Jamie asked.

"Not after us so much as Captain Deadmon himself," Mr. Pye returned. "Hawke's a brute and a bully. He's determined to go into the history books as the worst of all pirates. He envies Captain Deadmon's fame. His sure way to everlasting infamy is to be known as the man who overcame Captain Octavius Deadmon."

"Besides," said Wicks, "he's plain greedy. See, Jamie, everybody thinks there's great treasure aboard the *Betty.*"

They had reached the docks and climbed down into the pinnace, Mr. Pye taking the tiller this time. They cast off and the pinnace nosed around as Wicks ran the sail up. The wind was now to their left. Since they were more or less running against it rather than before it, the pinnace was trickier to handle.

As the boat came about, Mr. Pye said, "Wicks is right. Most people think that the *Betty* must be scuppers-deep in golden coins, emeralds, and rubies."

"She isn't?" Jamie asked. He sat amidships, his bundle of new clothing beside him.

"'Ware the sail," Sharkey said, and Jamie bent as the boom swept around and over him. "Nay, lad, the sailors of the *Betty* have better sense than to clutter her up with gold and jewels. Oh, we've taken treasure in our time, but we've been saving souls, eh, Davy Wicks?"

"Right you are, Ned," said Wicks from the bow. "The boys have put all their money in banks, where it's safe and sound."

" 'Course," Sharkey said, "they do favor different kinds o' banks."

"Aye," Wicks agreed. "Some there is that puts their money in gravel banks and some puts it in sand banks. Me, I bury mine in a good solid clay bank."

"But," Mr. Pye pointed out, "you all have maps to your buried treasure about you or in your berths. I daresay Roger Hawke would be glad to get his hands on them."

Sharkey's huge jaw dropped. "Thunder! You're right, Mr. Pye. I never thought o' that."

They were heading out of the harbor. Looking around the mast, Jamie could see the *Betty* anchored in the lee of the offshore rocks two or three miles away.

"Sir?" Jamie said in a small voice. "Just who is Hawke?"

Mr. Sharkey rumbled, "Mr. Pye's too much the gentleman to speak o' him. But I'll tell ye. Ye've heard o' Tradd? Bloody Tradd, they called him?"

Jamie recalled tales of the pirate with the flowing inky locks and the great blue-black beard, the man who cut enemies down like pork. "Yes."

"Well, Tradd were a child to Hawke. They do say that Hawke invented the Jolly Roger, and that it's named for him, but 'tis the other way around, I fancy. When he went in for piracy, Hawke changed his name from John or Bill or whatever it were to Roger. Anyhow, he's a desperate pirate and never takes prisoners, 'less they be ransomable. If he takes a common seaman, why, 'tis the plank for him, and never a chance to join or die."

Wicks had turned in the bows and was leaning back. "Aye. Nobody rightly knows where he was born. Some says Britolak, and some the West Countries, and some do say the devil himself spawned Hawke."

"I don't believe that," Sharkey said. "For there's the tale of his first murder. They say Hawke knifed his own father when he was twelve—Hawke, I mean, I don't know how old the father was—and stole the old man's ketch. Later he sold his mother to South Sea cannibals as the entree for one o' their pagan feasts. Anyhow, for twenty year he's been the scourge o' the seas, taking any vessel he fancies."

Wicks nodded. "He leads seven hundred scurvy pirates, in dozens o' ships. 'Tis my opinion they follow him because they fear him. 'Course, he does pile up heaps o' treasure too."

Mr. Pye, in the stern sheets, had remained silent. Suddenly he spoke: "What the devil's the matter with the ship?"

Jamie craned around the mast again. The *Betty* had raised anchor and was under sail, making off to the southeast. "She's running away," he said.

Wicks turned around in the bow. "Cap'n Deadmon must be bringing her about to come and fetch us off. She—oh, no. To starboard, Mr. Pye!"

As the first mate turned his head, Jamie also looked to the right. Just coming around a rocky headland was the prow of a sloop as black as pitch, with yellow trim on the rails. She seemed to be making for the *Betty*.

Mr. Pye's voice shook with fury: "It's Hawke's men. It's the *Flying Terror* herself!"

At that moment a puff of dirty white smoke billowed from the bow of the schooner. A couple of seconds later a dull double *boom!* rolled over the water.

"Blazes!" shouted Wicks from the bow. "She's firing at—"

But at that moment the sea erupted around them, and Jamie tumbled into cold water. He fought his way to the surface and came up gasping. The pinnace, her sail tattered, heeled around, and Wicks yelled something. Past the pinnace, the sloop glided swiftly over the water, heading not for them but for the *Betty*. As Jamie blinked the stinging salt water from his eyes, he saw the puff of smoke as Hawke's men fired their cannon again.

CHAPTER 6

The *Flying Terror*

Fortunately Jamie was barefoot, and with only his breeches and shirt to encumber him, he swam easily. He saw that despite a hole in the sail, the men aboard the pinnace were managing her well enough. They headed for him, angling to pass to his left. Jamie trod water as the boat boomed on.

Ned Sharkey leaned over the side, his eyes lighting up when he caught sight of Jamie. He stretched, and Jamie felt the seaman's huge hand close over his left arm. With a grunt Sharkey snatched him into the boat. "Are ye all right, lad?" the big man asked.

"No harm done," Jamie said. "Why are you shaking?"

"Why, Jamie," Wicks said, "ye could've drowned!"

"I can swim," Jamie protested. The look of astonishment exchanged by Wicks and Sharkey was Jamie's first inkling that not one in a dozen sailors could swim, and that their great terror was falling overboard into the unknown fathoms of the sea.

"We're coming about," said Mr. Pye at the tiller.

The pinnace lumbered as Mr. Pye made the turn. Water sloshed over their feet, and Wicks and Sharkey bailed with their hats. "What happened?" Jamie asked as the tattered sail swung round and partly filled with wind.

Pye said, "A near miss grazed the gunwale." Jamie saw that not twelve inches from his knee a splintered half-moon had been bitten out of the boat's side. "That tossed you out and made us ship water. At the same time, a charge of grape hit the sail. We thought you'd been shot."

Wicks tossed a last capful of water overboard, straightened up to peer forward, and cried out, "We'll never close with the *Betty* now."

Pye set his jaw. Jamie leaned over and saw the two ships well past the black scattering of rocks. The *Betty*'s starboard guns billowed to life. He might have counted to ten slowly before the sound thundered across the waves. White spouts of water burst short of the *Flying Terror,* and Wicks shouted out, "Missed, by thunder. I'll wager the villain has deflecting magic, and the *Betty* ain't close enough to overcome it."

"Get off, Captain Deadmon," Pye said between clenched teeth. "Don't hang back for us, but get away!"

The black ship swung about, taking advantage of the wind. It was almost parallel to the *Betty* when Jamie saw more puffs of smoke. To his horror the fore topgallant sail of the *Betty* suddenly collapsed in a tangle of rope and canvas. "She's hit!"

"Deadmon's waiting for us," Pye said, pounding a fist on his knee. "He can't outmaneuver the *Terror* with the wind against him. And we can't get past the *Terror* to reach him."

The *Betty* fired again and this time to some effect, for holes appeared in the gaff sail of the *Terror* and the shot splashed into the water on the far side of the enemy ship. "Take that!" Wicks shouted. "There's gunner Fletcher's own magic a-workin', lads." But even Jamie could see that the *Betty* had taken more damage than she had inflicted. The pirate sloop turned, training her starboard guns on the stern of Deadmon's ship.

The pinnace wallowed, its damaged sail flapping, almost directly north-northeast of the two ships, with the wind practically in their face. The sail luffed as Pye tacked, trying to get closer, but the *Betty,* on the same heading as they, drew away faster than they could come on.

A sudden thought came to Jamie. "Sir," he shouted, "could the *Betty* outrun the *Terror* with a following wind?"

"No question!" Pye yelled back. "If you've ever whistled true, Jamie, whistle now. Whistle, for your soul!"

Mr. Sharkey stopped his bailing to look round in astonishment as Jamie piped the clear notes of a jaunty old hornpipe. "In the Teeth of the Northeast Gale," it was called, and despite the fact that his heart was thumping in his throat, Jamie whistled it loud and strong:

I've spent long years upon the sea,
Long seasons under sail;
   But the grandest ride I ever took
   Was in the teeth of the northeast gale.

"Are ye daft?" Sharkey roared.

"Belay, Mr. Sharkey," Pye ordered, clapping a hand to hold his hat in place. "Jamie knows what he's about."

Wicks bellowed, "The wind's swingin' around!"

Jamie whistled harder. The southwestern breeze had died at the first notes, and now stiff blasts sprang up exactly opposite, a northeast wind. Far ahead of them the *Betty*'s sails filled in the fresh new gusts and the *Terror* wallowed, almost overwhelmed by the sudden change.

The clear sky darkened with scudding gray clouds as the northeast wind truly became a gale, raising whitecaps on the water. The pinnace's ripped sail grew taut as the waves surged higher. By the end of the tune, the pinnace was bucking and plunging, and Mr. Pye struggled to keep her heading.

They skimmed dangerously close to the black rocks, boiling white with foam as the gray breakers surged over them. As they rose to the top of the next wave, Jamie saw the *Betty* flying ahead of the gale with the *Terror* hopelessly behind. "She's away, sir!" he shouted in triumph.

But his joy was short-lived. Though Pye managed to skirt the rocks—so close that spray from the waves breaking over them drenched the men in the boat—the pinnace was drawing closer to the black sloop. Now Jamie could see a cluster of sailors in the bow swinging a swivel gun around, and this time when they fired it, Jamie heard the sound at the same instant he saw the flash.

The mast cracked and the sail collapsed. Thrown sideways, Jamie felt the pinnace lurch and take on more water. Then Sharkey pushed the broken mast away and cut the sail free. Jamie struggled up from the deck in water nearly knee-deep, and he began to bail frantically with his hands. Salt stung his eyes, but he could see that the mast had splintered six feet above his head. The sloop bore down on them, beating against the wind.

"Curse it," Sharkey said. "The lines all went over with the mast. And me with nary firearm nor cutlass."

"Steady," Pye ordered. "They'll take us, but the *Betty* escaped. For your lives do not let them know we're of the *Betty*'s crew, and you, Sharkey, keep still about your rope magic. If the rogues believe us townsmen, they may see more profit in ransoming us than in feeding the sharks."

The sloop hove to, men swung a gig over her side, and within a few seconds they had come alongside the pinnace and had made lines fast. The gig held five men, and two of them had pistols trained on the *Betty*'s men. Mr. Pye surrendered his saber, the two sailors their knives, and all of them were hustled up a rope ladder and aboard the *Terror*. Ned Sharkey grabbed the bundle of Jamie's clothes last of all and carried it aboard with him.

Jamie's heart sank as they came on deck. Two of the *Terror*'s men fell on the bundle and tore it apart, swearing mightily when all they found was clothing and shoes. "Nary a bit of swag!" one of them shouted, shaking a left shoe at Pye. "Just more bloody prisoners t' feed!"

One of the men from the gig prodded Jamie hard in the back, and the boy and the others marched to the bow of the ship. There a burly man stood with legs braced wide apart, a brass telescope raised to his face.

"Cap'n," said the man behind Jamie, "We caught 'em."

The captain wore a long blue coat, its trim all torn away and its fabric stained. He growled in his throat, dropped the telescope into a side pocket, and turned. His face was ugly and scowling. His brows, like his hair, were a grizzled iron gray, and a two-days' beard glinted on his chin. A livid scar began at the left corner of his mouth and ran up his cheek, disappearing beneath a black patch over his left eye. "So the big fish got away, but ye netted four minnows." His good right eye glared madly. "Splinter your bones and spill your blood, but we've lost a grand prize while hanging about to capture your miserable hides. Ye'd better be worth it."

"We are poor," Mr. Pye said, quite easily. "Your men left hardly anything of worth in the town, Captain ... ?"

"Creighton," the captain snapped. Jamie saw Sharkey suddenly stand straighter. "More miserable landlubbers, are ye?"

"They had clothes for the boy," the man behind Jamie volunteered. "Like he was puttin' to sea."

Creighton turned his glaring eye on Jamie. "What o' that?"

Mr. Pye answered again: "The boy has served on fishing craft before. It's an honorable trade, is fishing."

Creighton spat over the rail. "Urvis, ye harebrain," he said. "Bringin' aboard a worthless fisherboy instead o' a fit prize. What'll Hawke say?"

"How was I to know?" Urvis—the man holding the pistol against Jamie's back near his left kidney—whined. "I thunk they might be Deadmon's men."

"Well, ye thunk wrong, ye lubber. So, fisher-folk, be there anybody ashore as might pay a gulden or two for your return? Or should we chop ye into bait?"

Mr. Pye said, "Oh, we're worth a coin or two."

Creighton stared at him with animal cunning. "We may get a bit more," he said in a dangerously quiet tone. "Ye talks more like a eddicated gentleman. A schoolmaster or p'rhaps a magistrate? We might get more'n one coin, I fancy." He turned to his own men. "Clap 'em in irons, and when this bloody wind changes, we'll get a deppytation in to bargain for these sprats."

"Back in th' cabin wi' the womenfolk?" asked Urvis.

"What? No cabin for them—below decks, ye fool. Avast, though! Have ye turned 'em out?"

Turning out proved to be a thorough search. Jamie, who had nothing in his pockets, was a disappointment to them. Wicks had a few coppers, and Sharkey wore a curious silver ring which they took, but Mr. Pye's purse was the great prize, containing six pieces of gold, some silver, and a few copper penans and brass quartrings.

"That's mine," Creighton said, and with some grumbling the sailor who had found the purse inside Pye's coat turned it over. The complaining sailors then hustled the four captives down the forward companionway.

"Women and kiddies," one of them said with a snarl. "I don't know what piratin's come to. Along with ye, now! Lively, lively!" He shoved Jamie so hard that the boy stumbled. They descended through the forecastle, down a hatchway, to a spot well below the waterline. It was a gloomy, spare passageway that seemed to run the length of the ship along the starboard side, but it was so dark they could see little.

Jamie felt sick at the stench of bilge and the rolling of the ship. But he uttered no complaint as the sailors locked an iron bracelet to his left wrist, ran a chain attached to it through a staple affixed to a rib of the sloop, and snapped the other end of the chain to a cuff around Mr. Pye's right wrist. Wicks and Sharkey were similarly treated. "There's bracelets for ye," one of the sailors said, patting Wicks mockingly on the cheek. "Almos' as pretty jew'ry as the dainty lass in th' back cabin wore." The other sailors laughed.

Another pirate, carrying a lantern, clambered down and hurled the bundle of Jamie's clothes at the captives' feet. "If ye gets cold, rip these for blankets, lads." His laughter gurgled into a consumptive cough.

Creighton's men checked the cuffs, tugging so hard at the chain that they made Jamie's wrist bones grind together. Satisfied, the pirates began to leave. The last one, armed with a pistol thrust into his belt and a musket in his hand, remained at the foot of the ladder. "Leave us some light," he said as the others started up.

"Here," one of them said, holding out the lantern. It contained one dim candle.

"The devil take ye for his dinner, how can I hold that thing? Fix it up, Fritz, afore ye leaves."

With ill grace Fritz hooked the lantern over a hanging chain before he went up the ladder. Swinging and flickering, the candle provided scant light and cast dark heaving shadows.

"Mr. Pye—" Jamie began.

"Silence between decks!" snapped the sentry.

Pye frowned and shook his head. Jamie fell silent.

The chain holding them together was strong and only four feet long. The iron staple was as thick as Jamie's little finger, and with a guard watching them he had no hope of even trying to pull it free. The chain was not long enough to allow them both to sit down; one had to stand while the other rested. Mr. Pye let Jamie have the first turn, and the boy sat for perhaps two hours before he gave the first mate a chance to ease his legs.

In the meantime, a new guard, distinctly the worse for drink, relieved their surly sentry and put a new candle in the lantern. Jamie gathered from the violent motion of the ship that the wind was still strong. As the rocking lulled their guard, the man's eyes blinked and drooped, and finally he sat down at the foot of the ladder. Mr. Pye cautiously stood, holding the slack of the chain in his hand so it would not clink. He leaned close to Jamie to whisper, "How long will your wind blow, lad?"

Jamie said, "I don't know, sir. I whistled hard—I suppose it's good for the night."

"That gives us some little time. Headache?"

Jamie blinked in surprise. "No, sir. Not at all."

"I thought not, since you did magic because you wanted to this time. See if we can loosen this chain."

Together they strained against their bond, but as Jamie feared, the chain proved too strong. "Blast," Pye puffed. "Can you slip your hand out of the cuff?"

Jamie tried, but the steel wristlet had been put on so tightly that he could not slide the band off. Muffled sounds told him that Sharkey and Wicks were also testing their bonds.

"That's enough," Pye whispered. "Don't tear your skin off. We shall have to think of something else."

From off to his right Sharkey grunted, and Jamie heard a squeal like an anguished pig. The sentry started, yawned, and rose, rubbing his eyes. The prisoners fell quiet again. More time passed, and a sailor came down the ladder with a dry sea biscuit apiece for the captives, plus a leather flask of brackish-tasting water that they had to pass from hand to hand. Jamie chewed the biscuit with difficulty, for he had swallowed salt water and his throat burned with thirst that the warm water in the flask seemed only to aggravate.

"Here," complained the sentry, "ain't I to have no relief? It be time."

"Avast," the other said. "Every man Jack is required to run afore this cursed wind. Ye're the least handy of 'em all, Stott, so ye've drawn sentry duty."

Stott cursed the other man up the ladder, then turned a baleful eye on the captives. "I'll have a go o' rum, anyhow," he said, more to himself than to them. He looked craftily up the ladder, then climbed up, his musket making his moves awkward.

As soon as he was out of sight, Sharkey said, "Mr. Pye! We nearly worked the hook out. With a bit more muscle, we could do it. Can you get close enough to lend a hand?"

"Jamie, give me all the slack you can."

Jamie put his hand right beside the iron staple, and Mr. Pye pulled the chain through, making an unholy clatter. Fortunately the ship was making a great deal of noise, ropes groaning, waves dashing, and cargo shifting. Mr. Pye strained even more, and Jamie bit his lip as the chain jerked hard at the wrist-cuff.

"There," Pye grunted. "Pull this way, lads. Now try to turn it."

Jamie heard a sudden cracking, and Wicks gasped.

Pye's voice held triumph: "That's done it, my hearties! It's far enough out to slip the chain off. Now help us."

Sharkey said, "Half a tick." The chain eased, letting Jamie drop his hand. Jamie's heart began to pound as he heard the jangle of chain off to his right. Then Sharkey and Wicks, their faces grim in the uncertain, pitching light, moved over. Though still chained together, at least they were free of the staple. Sharkey grabbed Jamie's side of the chain. "Same fastening as ours. All pull together. One, two, three!"

Jamie heaved as hard as he could, and the staple gave slightly. He could now see that it was nothing more than a very large nail with the head cut off, bent into a *J* shape and pounded into the rib. They pulled again, and the shorter end of the hook screeched out of the wood.

"That's enough," Pye said. "Back to your places, men!"

The others slipped their chain back into their own bent hook just in time, for a clatter of boots on the ladder told them their captor was returning. Stott cradled a bottle of rum in his left arm. Settling into a corner, the guard took a deep swallow.

Jamie's heart was still racing, for in his mind he pictured all sorts of desperate action: their rushing the guard, seizing the weapons, fighting their way topside. But none of this happened. Instead, they all remained quiet until the guard slumped into sleep, snoring loudly.

Mr. Pye fished in his breast pocket and finally found a small notebook. "Lucky no one wanted this," he whispered to Jamie. "See if you can seize the lantern when it swings closest, lad, and bring it to me."

Moving to the limit of the chain, Jamie reached up, missed, waited, and then succeeded in grasping the swinging lantern. He managed to remove it from its chain without putting out the light and offered it to Mr. Pye.

"Hold it for me, if you please. Ah—nice and sooty." Mr. Pye dipped his forefinger in the open top of the lantern and blackened it in the soot that had accumulated there. As Jamie watched in puzzlement, Pye made a mark in the center of one of the notebook pages. Evidently not satisfied, he repeated the process again and again, until he had made a black circle two finger-widths across.

"That will do," he said. He quickly folded the paper envelope-fashion, then reached for the lantern. Tilting it, he allowed wax to drip on the fold of the paper. After a moment he pressed his thumb into the warm wax to seal his strange message. "Now, lad," he whispered. "Hang this up without waking our friend."

That was difficult, but Jamie rehung the lantern. "Now what?" he whispered.

"What time would you say it is, lad?"

"I don't know. Evening, surely."

"Then," said Pye, "the best thing for us is to get some rest. Come morning, we may be able to do a thing or two. I can stir things up, but it's hard to know just what we can accomplish without getting ourselves and the ladies killed."

"The ladies? The prisoners they spoke of?"

"Aye, lad. Some poor wenches these blackguards have kidnapped, from the way they talk." Pye's voice dropped even lower. "Well, it may be that trying to escape will only get us killed, but better a quick death for us all—and particularly for the wenches—than suffering at the hands of these villains. Try to rest now."

Despite Mr. Pye's cheery advice, Jamie did snatch a few minutes of sleep, though the night crawled by on hands and knees. Sometime well after sundown a younger fellow relieved Stott, but even he would not allow talking.

It must have been past midnight when Jamie became aware that the motion of the ship had diminished. Evidently his gale had blown itself out, and the ship was riding easier. Again he tried to sleep, and he succeeded to the extent of dozing for a few moments at a time, always to jerk himself awake with a start.

The guard changed again, and then again: four-hour tours, Jamie decided. At last, close to daybreak, their surly friend Stott came back, red-eyed and grumbling. It did not take long for him to sit at the foot of the ladder and nod off.

When he was snoring, Mr. Pye leaned close to Jamie. "Lad, do you remember the deck? Was there not a gig lashed down to starboard of the mizzen?"

"Aye," Jamie whispered. "Forward of the aft companionway."

"That is our way out," Pye returned. "It will be a desperate chance."

With a glance at their guard, Pye loosened the chain and beckoned Jamie to come with him. The other two sailors were on their feet. They put all their heads together, and Pye asked, "Mr. Sharkey, whereabout would the powder be kept?"

Sharkey rubbed his unshaven jaw. "I expect just aft, sir."

Pye nodded. "This is a long chance, my lads, and I wish I could make the odds more favorable, but here's what I'm planning." In a few words he sketched in his intentions. Jamie felt cold, but he could offer no better alternative, and so he nodded his agreement with the others.

Then he and Pye returned to their spot. Pye shouted, "Hi! You, guard!"

The man leaped to his feet, bringing his musket to bear. "Need a touch o' my fist to shut ye up, is that it?"

"Call the young fellow back, sir," Pye ordered. "I've decided to give in."

Stott's ugly face contracted in a great effort at thought. "Eh? What d'ye mean?"

Pye produced the sealed paper. "The young fellow seems a decent sort. I've written this letter to some friends ashore, and they'll ransom us, I'll be bound. And I'm sure the young fellow would gain the favor of your captain by taking him the news."

"Him? Why should he get the good luck, eh?"

Pye shrugged. "He was kind to us. He gave us an extra sip of water when we were thirsty. For that I think he should have some of the thousand guldens, don't you?"

Stott's bleary eyes went small and piggy. "Thousand gulden?"

"Aye, and all he has to do is take this to the captain."

The guard put down his musket and drew a pistol from his belt. He cocked the hammer and edged toward them, the muzzle of the pistol aimed at Mr. Pye's breast. "Give it here," he said.

Pye sounded genuinely hurt: "No, you misunderstand. I want the young fellow who gave us—"

The pirate snatched the paper. "A thousand gulden, eh?"

Pye straightened. "If it is unopened, of course. I took the precaution of sealing it—"

"And who give ye the wax?" Dim cunning dawned in those squinting eyes. "Ah, I see. Precious little Alex, as gives ye water. We'll see what Cap'n Creighton has to say about these doings. A thousand gulden!" With an evil chuckle, the guard snatched up his musket and climbed the ladder.

"Now, quickly," Pye said as soon as he was gone. He and Jamie and the other two slipped their chains free of the hooks and Pye reached down the candle, replenished for the third or fourth time but already burned low.

He and Jamie crept aft along the gallery. They found a locker at the foot of the mainmast, and stacked around it, lashed down, kegs of powder. Sharkey snapped the ropes free of the kegs, Pye picked one cask up, and with Jamie holding the lantern they returned forward.

"By the bow, sir," said Sharkey. He and Wicks stood at the foot of the ladder, ready for anyone descending. "Give us as much time as ye can spare."

"I will, lads. Here's to luck!"

Jamie followed the first mate forward. The bulkhead curved sharply inward close to the bow. Pye wedged the keg between the forward bulkhead and a rib, and then with a couple of kicks he partially stove in the lid, so that a black cascade of powder leaked out. "Carefully," he said, taking the lantern. He removed the candle, stood it in a pool of its own wax, and then scraped powder around the base. Jamie held his breath. If a spark touched the powder. . . .

But Pye was careful, leaving the flame three-quarters of an inch above the powder. When the candle burned down, the gunpowder would catch. An instant later the keg would explode.

"Now," Pye said, "let's—" From far overhead came the sound of curses and the clank of steel on steel. Pye grinned. "The letter has been delivered!"

They hurried back to the ladder, no longer caring that their chain clanked. "Up, boys," Pye said in the darkness.

"Wait," Wicks said in a desperate whisper. "Listen!"

Jamie heard a heavy tread coming down the ladder.

Ned Sharkey took up the slack chain in his huge right hand. "Caught between fire and the devil, eh? I'll show 'em a thing or two afore I'm done," he said.

And as battle raged up on deck, the sound of heavy boots came closer and closer.

CHAPTER 7

The Last of the *Terror*

The four of them drew back, their chains clinking. Jamie held his breath as the footsteps approached.

Gooseflesh prickled his arms. In the gloom a disembodied foot descended from the highest rung of the ladder to the next. Wicks gasped, and Jamie felt Mr. Pye go tense.

The foot hesitated. Stopped, it looked less footlike and more birdlike, and from it came a querulous voice: "Ahoy, below! Who goes there?"

Jamie breathed at last. "Squok!"

Sharkey muttered, "'Tis only the ship's parrot."

With a ruffle of feathers Squok shook himself. "Only the parrot! That's gratitude! Who risked flying weary sea-miles and coming aboard this plaguey pirate ship—"

"You sounded like a sailor," Jamie said.

Squok opened his beak and produced a sound just like that of a boot tramping on a ladder rung. "Thought I'd pass unnoticed if I sounded like a member of the crew," the bird said, puffing with pride.

"Birdbrain," Wicks said. "Ye could've come on silent—"

"There's no time," Mr. Pye said. "We're escaping."

"And I've come to help." Squok leaped to Jamie's shoulder. "The *Betty* has nipped around and now stands four sea-miles off behind a headland, waiting to ambush the *Terror* as soon as I return." Jamie reached to tickle his chest, and the iron links clattered. "Chained?" Squok asked. "You'll never make it chained. There's a fellow asleep in his hammock up in the forecastle yonder, and on a peg at the head of his bunk hangs a ring of keys."

"Bring them," Mr. Pye said.

"Too heavy and noisy. But avast! Stand by." Squok flapped his wings, grumbled low in his chest, and suddenly roared, "Shiver my timbers! Out o' that hammock, and lively! I wants the keys, ye lubber!" Squok's mimicry of Captain Creighton was frighteningly exact.

"Aye, sir!" there was a patter of footsteps above.

"Throw down the keys, dog! Then topside wi' ye!"

The keys rattled down, and Sharkey caught them. They heard the sailor clambering up the ladder.

"Quick," Pye said. "Unlock these bracelets, Mr. Sharkey."

Sharkey found the right key, and the chain clattered from Mr. Pye's wrist, then from Jamie's. As Sharkey unlocked his and Wicks's bonds, Mr. Pye climbed the ladder. Jamie followed, with Squok reeling and flapping to stay on the boy's shoulder.

Pye reached the head of the ladder and cracked the hatch. Dawn light, dazzling after the gloom of the ship's belly, spilled in, along with shouts and the clang of steel. "Blast," Mr. Pye said. "They're dueling in the waist. We can't get past 'em."

The ship leaped as a tremendous explosion ripped through her. It almost shook Jamie off the ladder, but behind him Wicks put a steadying hand on his back. Squok did tumble off, got a painful grip at Jamie's waist, and scrambled up the boy's back and to his shoulder. Jamie's ears rang.

"That's got their attention," Pye said as feet pounded on the deck all around.

Smoke poured from below decks. "She's alight! We got to get out, sir," said Sharkey from below.

"All right, lads, now!"

Pye flung the hatch open and scrambled on deck, Jamie following. The *Flying Terror* listed to starboard, and gray billows streaked with crimson flame spewed from her bows. The ship had fallen into the eye of the wind, the sails luffing, and choking smoke rolled straight back along her decks. Jamie's eyes streamed, but in the reek Creighton's men, similarly stricken, overlooked him and the others.

Pye led the way aft. Just as they reached the gig, a sailor stopped and stared at them. It was Alex, one of the guards from the night before, and with an oath he drew his cutlass.

But Ned Sharkey stepped forth to meet him. Sharkey had not dropped the manacles that had bound him and Wicks. He swung the chain in a whistling circle. Alex, raising his cutlass, was not ready. The chain clanged against his head, cartwheeling him into a senseless jumble of arms and legs.

Wicks stooped to retrieve the cutlass the pirate had dropped as Sharkey rolled the unconscious man over and drew two pistols from his belt. "Primed and loaded," he said, handing one of the weapons to Pye. "We'll get the gig, sir. You see to the other prisoners back in the cabin."

Jamie had almost forgotten the other captives. Squok coughed in the thickening smoke as the boy followed Pye into the aft companionway. The narrow corridor had cabins on either side, and Jamie tried the starboard ones, Pye the port. The second door Jamie rattled was locked.

A woman's voice screamed, "Go away, you scoundrels!"

"Mr. Pye!" Jamie shouted. "Here!" Louder, he called, "We've come to rescue you—we're not pirates!"

"Stand away!" Pye bellowed. Jamie leaped back as the first mate braced his back against the port bulkhead and gave the door a flat-footed kick. The cabin door sprang inward.

"Come on!" Pye shouted. He reached inside and pulled out a handsome middle-aged woman.

"Wait," she cried. "Come, dear. These nice men are saving us."

Jamie blinked. "Mrs. Llewellen! Princess!"

Mr. Pye said, "I'm glad you're all acquainted, but right now we really must run. On deck, all!"

The princess, her brown hair disheveled and her dress torn

and bedraggled, grasped Jamie's hand and he led her onto the smoky deck. They heard the sound of blade ringing against blade, and when they burst into the open they saw Wicks furiously exchanging blows with a much larger man. Wicks's sword flashed, and the pirate gave way until he was against the starboard bulkhead.

The list had increased to thirty degrees, and the tall pirate lost his balance and tumbled backward. The last glimpse Jamie had of him was of a pair of dirty bare feet flipping into the air. A splash marked his end.

Sharkey's rope magic had loosed the gig. "Help me!"

Pye, Wicks, and Sharkey heaved the gig overboard. With the cutlass Wicks slashed one of the stays and tossed the free end over. He swung down it and into the boat.

"You, lad," said Pye, boosting Jamie over the rail. The ship listed so badly that the gig rode almost directly beneath Jamie. He swung down and landed in the bow as Squok took off and flew away.

Pye lifted the princess over the bulkhead. Wicks and Jamie reached up for her—to his embarrassment, Jamie's hands went under the hem of her tattered dress and he found himself hugging her bare knees—and they lowered her into the boat. She sat panting on the bow thwart beside Jamie, clinging to him.

Mrs. Llewellen surprised Jamie by climbing down the rope unassisted into the stern. From above, Sharkey yelled, "Creighton!"

Jamie could not clearly see what was happening on deck, but Pye spun and fired his pistol at some target forward and out of sight. Sharkey picked up the first mate by the scruff of his neck and dropped him into the stern of the gig. Then the big man swung down himself, landing amidships.

Only then did Jamie see that Sharkey was burdened. He had a pair of oars under his left arm, and in his left hand he grasped the bundle of clothing they had bought in town the day before. Sharkey settled himself on the center thwart, pushed away from the hull, and fitted the oars. With one sweep the gig sprang away from the sinking *Terror*.

"Missed the beggar," said Pye from the stern.

"There, sir," Sharkey said soothingly. "Ye would've stayed behind to cover our escape—I know you, stem to stern. Beggin' your pardon, sir, none of us wanted that."

"Dear?" cried Mrs. Llewellen, craning to look over Sharkey's shoulder at Amelia.

The princess, beside Jamie, said, "I'm quite all right, Nanny. A rescue! How very exciting!"

"Thank heavens. I don't know what I should tell your da and mum."

From the bow, Wicks interrupted: "Sit easy, ma'am. We're precious near overloaded—take easy strokes, Ned!"

Jamie glanced down and saw that only three or four inches of freeboard appeared above the water. When he looked back at the *Terror,* his heart thudded. On the deck stood Captain Creighton, his arm raised and a pistol aimed their way. He fired, but the ball went wide and splashed into the sea yards past the gig.

"That awful man." Amelia reached to take Jamie's hand.

Creighton cried out some order, and a man armed with a musket ran to his side. "Look out, Mr. Sharkey," warned Pye from the stern. "He'll aim for you!"

"Get the pistol from my belt," Sharkey said. "Nobody could hit him at this distance, but see if ye can distract him."

"I can't reach you—" Pye began.

But Mrs. Llewellen could. She snatched the pistol up, turned, raised her left arm, balanced the pistol barrel in the crook of her elbow, and squeezed the trigger.

The pistol barked, and on the deck the musket flew to pieces. The marksman danced away, shaking his hand and yelping, while Creighton screamed more orders.

"Well shot, madam!" Pye cried out in undisguised admiration.

"Hmpf," sniffed Mrs. Llewellen. "He is lucky that I'm a forgiving sort, or I would have put the ball between his eyes."

"Bless me," grunted Sharkey, pulling them away from the *Ter-*

ror. "Begging your pardon, ma'am, but how did a lady like you learn to shoot so straight?"

"Well," Mrs. Llewellen said, trying to smooth her disheveled hair, "a girl should learn how to protect herself."

Amelia trembled. "Oh, look," she said.

Pye stared behind them. They were well away from the *Terror.* The ship was going down by the bows, and its deck was tilted toward them at an angle of at least forty degrees. Creighton, his saber raised, was forcing one of the men to swing the swivel gun toward them.

Pye said, "Sharkey, stand by to back water when I tell you, but carefully, or you'll swamp us."

"Aye," Sharkey growled. "Pity we ain't got another pistol."

"Steady—steady—"

Cannon boomed, but not from the *Terror.* Jamie looked over his shoulder and yelled with joy. The *Betty* had hove into sight, broadside to the *Terror*, and had fired her guns.

The rounds ripped into the *Terror* close to the waterline. Timbers flew, raising a spray of foam. The sinking ship reeled, the man at the swivel gun lost his footing, and the gun discharged in the air, sending shot through the *Terror*'s mainsail.

"Deadmon's done her!" Mr. Pye shouted in triumph. "That was Creighton's last shot, by thunder!"

Wicks said, "Two points starboard, Ned, and pull for the *Betty.*"

"Aye, aye, Mr. Wicks, sir," returned Sharkey with a laugh. "Mr. Pye, what say ye we let this former cabin boy be cap'n o' this here gig?"

"Wonderful suggestion," Mr. Pye said.

Jamie glanced around. Wicks was blushing a brilliant scarlet, but a grin covered his whole face. "In that case," he said, "my orders stand. Pull away, my hearty!"

"Aye, aye." Sharkey chuckled again.

Other boats deserted the *Flying Terror.* Jamie counted five, all heavily loaded with sailors. One, a pinnace, broke out its sail, and in its stern he could see the hulking figure of Captain Creighton.

The *Terror*'s bows plunged beneath the waves. Her stern lifted until the ship finally stood vertical, and then she slipped under the surface, leaving behind a wrack of swirling timbers, barrels, and canvas.

"Oh," Amelia said. "The ship quite disappeared. It was almost like a conjuring trick."

Jamie swallowed and nodded. Though he had no cause to wish luck to Captain Creighton or his cutthroat crew, it was sobering to see how fast the ocean could claim a ship.

The *Betty* made toward them, and in a few minutes they came alongside the ship. Jamie helped Amelia aboard, and Mr. Pye followed, assisting Mrs. Llewellen. As soon as he was aboard, Wicks hurried forward and climbed the foremast stays. The others went aft, where Captain Deadmon, with Squok on his shoulder, stood by the wheel.

"There ye are, lad," said Sharkey, dropping the bundle of clothing on the deck with a plop.

"You didn't have to hold on to that," Jamie protested.

Sharkey's chest swelled. "No ship I sailed ever lost cargo to a scurvy crew o' pirates. And now I got dooties to do." Sharkey hurried away just as the captain turned toward them.

"We have returned, sir," Pye said with a smart salute.

"And brought visitors," Deadmon said in his usual lugubrious tones. "Welcome aboard, ladies."

Mrs. Llewellen gave him a doubtful look, but she curtsied. "Thank you, Captain. Your men have done us a welcome turn, and Princess Amelia of Laurel and I stand in your debt."

Deadmon inclined his head gravely. "Any unfortunate in the hands of Hawke or his men is more than welcome to my assistance, madam. But if you will pardon me, we still have business." The captain ordered Tallow to make for the pinnace, and the *Betty* changed course.

Squok flew to Jamie's shoulder. Amelia cried out in delight

and began to tickle him with her free hand, making Jamie realize that he was still holding her other hand. He let it go hastily.

"How did you distract Creighton?" Deadmon asked Pye.

"I tricked one of the crew into giving Creighton a letter," Pye said. "Except it wasn't a letter. The man tipped his captain the black spot."

Deadmon made a curious sound, something like the distant echo of gunshots. Jamie realized that he was laughing.

"Excuse me," said Mrs. Llewellen. "The black spot?"

Pye bowed. "The black spot, madam, is a pirate's notice to his captain that he is being challenged for the leadership of the crew. Our guard gave Creighton a folded paper. When the captain opened it, instead of a letter he saw a challenge. As I expected, Creighton did not wait for explanations. He must have attacked at once, and then the man had to defend himself. It made a temporary diversion."

"Oh," said Mrs. Llewellen. "How very resourceful, sir."

"He is that, madam," Deadmon said. "But I beg your pardon again, for there is the pinnace, and I mean to have a word with that rascally Creighton."

They followed him forward as he gave quiet orders. A crew stood by each starboard gun. Mr. Border held a large red megaphone, which he handed to Deadmon.

Deadmon raised the speaking tube to his lips. "Ahoy, the pinnace!" His sepulchral voice boomed across the water.

They were close enough so that Jamie could see Creighton's angry face turned in their direction. The left sleeve of his coat was torn away, and he wore a bloodstained bandage on his arm. He shook his right fist in their direction.

"Walter Creighton," Deadmon shouted, "you've interfered with my crew, sir, and you owe me a pinnace."

The crew of the overloaded pinnace cast wild glances at the *Betty*. Every cannon was aimed directly at their craft. Creighton put his good hand beside his mouth and raged, "Ye bloody old corpse! Ye've done for yourselves, d'ye hear? Hawke won't let none o' ye stay above water now!"

"Mr. Fletcher," Deadmon said to his gunner, "just remind Mr. Creighton who's in most danger of feeding the fishes."

Mr. Fletcher's drooping gray walrus mustache quivered upward. "Aye, aye!"

"Oh, sir," said Mrs. Llewellen. "Surely you would not sink them, unarmed as they are? They may be scoundrels, but—"

"Madam," said Pye, "pray watch."

The *Betty*'s guns roared, making Amelia jump and throw her arms around Jamie. Fountains of spray erupted all around the pinnace—but not a shot touched her. "There, you see?" Pye said, his quiet voice hardly penetrating the ringing in Jamie's ears. "Mr. Fletcher is a magician with a twelve-pounder."

The pinnace's crew made off with men even trying to row with their hands. "I'll bring Hawke to ye!" Creighton screamed. "Ye're naught but fish bait, d'ye hear?"

Deadmon tipped his hat ironically. Turning aft, he shouted, "You may come to larboard, Mr. Tallow."

"Aye, aye, sir!" Tallow called cheerily from the wheel. "Comin' to larboard, sir!"

Wicks had climbed back down, smiling and shaking his head. "We seen the fore-topgallant fall," he told Deadmon. "But ye've made her shipshape again, Cap'n."

"A new spar and fresh canvas, lad," Deadmon returned. "The old ship took little damage, but now the carpenter will have to knock together another pinnace."

"Look at 'em," Sharkey said. Creighton's boat had raised sail and was making all possible speed northward, and the other small boats had great ado to keep up. "Creighton cares a lot for his men, don't he?" He spat disdainfully over the side.

"Mr. Pye," said Mrs. Llewellen, laying a hand on his arm. "I know we haven't been introduced."

"Easily remedied," Pye said. "Jamie, lad, you know these ladies, I believe?"

"Oh!" Jamie disentangled himself from Amelia's arms and led the princess to her governess. "Mrs. Llewellen, Princess Amelia, this is Mr. Pye, the first mate of the *Betty,* and this is Captain

Octavius Deadmon, her master. Captain, Mr. Pye, uh, may I present Mrs. Llewellen, governess, and, uh, Amelia, the princess of the kingdom of Laurel."

Mr. Pye gave a grave bow. "I am honored, ladies."

"Oh," said Mrs. Llewellen, pressing her palms to her breast. "And so are we. Mr. Pye, we would be grateful if your ship could convey us safely to Laurel."

Pye's morose expression deepened. "There is a difficulty, madam," he said.

"Too true," added Deadmon. "Madam, unfortunately the wicked pirate Hawke and all his fleet stand to the north. If we try to make heading for Laurel, we are bound to run smack into him. You have already had a sample of the kind of hospitality he and his men extend."

Amelia shuddered. "Oh, Nanny, I couldn't stand those terrible men again," she said.

"Nor I," said Mrs. Llewellen. "But surely this is a fighting ship?"

"Aye, madam," Deadmon said, just a hint of pride creeping into his toneless voice. "She is. But Roger Hawke's ships hopelessly outnumber and outgun us. We dare not take the chance."

"I daresay," Pye put in, "that we could put the ladies ashore to the south?"

Deadmon nodded. "World's End, perhaps, or—"

"Oh, no," groaned Mrs. Llewellen. "Please, no. I should be quite giddy."

Pye looked baffled. "Then what are we to do, madam?"

Mrs. Llewellen sounded vexed to the point of tears: "Oh, I'm sure I don't know."

"Where are you going?" Amelia asked.

Pye looked to the Captain. Deadmon said, "Lady, we are venturing to the lair of a dragon, to plunder his hoard."

Amelia clapped her hands in glee. "Dragons!" she squealed. "Ooh, how lucky we are! Nanny, please, may we go?"

"Child," Mrs. Llewellen said. "These men do not want us underfoot, I'm sure—"

"On the contrary," Deadmon said. "You grace the ship with your presence, madam."

Pye took off his hat and bowed low. "My captain speaks truly. Were it my decision, I should not hesitate to ask you to join us. But it will be a dangerous voyage, and perhaps even a desperate one."

"Ooh," Amelia said again. "Please, Nanny? Please?"

Deadmon said, "We could keep you aboard temporarily. It would be best if we made our offing at once and headed for Windrose Island, getting the start of Hawke. But it's a voyage of a month, and we're likely to fall in with ships for Anglavon. You might transfer to one of them and so return safely home."

Mrs. Llewellen cast a despairing glance at Amelia's wild hair, at their torn and stained dresses. "La, sir, we're hardly fit for decent society." She put her hand to her lips and blinked at Mr. Pye. "Not saying, sir, that you yourself are not decent. I meant no offense."

"I took none, madam," said Mr. Pye in his melancholy way.

"But perhaps it would be best if we stayed aboard for some little time. I do feel safe here." She favored Mr. Pye with a winning smile.

"Then it's settled," Deadmon said. "We must find some accommodation for you."

"Sir," Pye said, "They may have my cabin. It's large enough, and I could swing a hammock in the stern cabin."

Deadmon nodded. "So be it. Welcome aboard, ladies. Now, please pardon me once more, for we must set sail."

"Come," Pye said, offering his arm to Mrs. Llewellen. "I'll show you to your quarters, and you can freshen up. We have some clothing aboard that might fit you—out of date, I fear, for it's from a Vrenkon ship that we took last year."

"Vrenkish fashions?" breathed Mrs. Llewellen. "La, Mr. Pye, I should hardly know how to wear them. Is that the famous Captain Deadmon, of whom I've heard such wonderful stories?"

"Madam, it is." They strolled aft arm in arm, with Jamie looking after them. Squok bit his ear.

"Ouch!" he cried, clapping a hand to his head. "What did you do that for—" he broke off. Amelia stood beside him in an expectant attitude.

"Well?" she asked with a tentative smile. "You didn't introduce yourself. Of course I remember you from the inn."

"Oh," he said. He gulped. Amelia's brown hair straggled loose over her shoulders, her dress had been torn around the hem, and her feet and legs were bare. She looked less like a princess than a country girl. "I'm Jamie Falconer," he said. "I, uh, ran away from the inn."

"Good for you," she said. "That Mr. Growdy treated you horribly, I know he did. And you saved the lovely parrot."

"You're very smart for a princess," Squok said.

Her smile turned sad. "I'm not, really. Mum and Da say I'm most awfully slow—" she broke off. "You talked!"

Squok preened himself.

"Oh, talk again!" she said. "Do!"

"He won't," Jamie said. "That's his way."

"Shows what you know," Squok said. "Princess, I think Jamie should give you his arm, don't you?"

"*Squok!*" Jamie bellowed.

Several of the sailors looked around at him, and Mr. Border, leaning on the rail, laughed aloud.

Feeling his face burn, Jamie bent his arm. Amelia gave a curtsy and put her hand through the crook of his elbow. With his free hand he picked up the bundle of clothing that Mr. Sharkey had rescued from the *Terror*. Perhaps he walked Amelia aft to the cabin rather quickly, but at that moment his only thought was to get her and himself out of sight of the crew of the *Betty*.

CHAPTER 8

Princess Amelia

That afternoon Mrs. Llewellen told a story that roused the indignation of every man who heard it. "We left the inn where dear little Jamie worked," the governess said (not noticing how Jamie squirmed at being called "dear"). "And the coach made very good speed until we came to a place where the road overlooks a steep bluff leading down to a round cove—"

"Black Hill Cove," a sailor put in. "A rare place for smugglers."

"As you say," Mrs. Llewellen sniffled. "Those horrid men were there. They robbed us of everything. Then one of them asked dear Amelia, 'Who be you, chuck?' And my dear girl said, 'I'm Princess Amelia of Laurel. Who are you, sir?'"

"A bad move, that," said the sailor.

A stupid move, Jamie added mentally.

"Well, the child is so innocent. At any rate, the pirates then decided they must kidnap her and hold her for ransom. I insisted that they take me too, for her care is my duty. Since then we've had not a decent morsel of food nor even a bath."

That could be remedied. The men offered the women choice tid-bits from the ship's larder, and they fetched hot water aft to the great cabin, where a tin bathtub afforded first Amelia, and then her governess, the chance to make themselves clean and fresh again.

Mrs. Llewellen's doubts about the suitability of Vrenkish fashions proved happily ungrounded. She found for herself a selection of demure black silk dresses that only wanted letting out in the bust to fit her. This operation she undertook with needle and thread ("A wonderfully handy woman," marveled Mr. Pye), and in less than a day she had a whole new wardrobe. On seeing her again, Captain Deadmon said she made "a fine trim craft of a female, fit to be a figurehead." Mr. Pye appeared to agree with the captain.

As for Amelia—well, clothing her proved to be a disaster, at least in Jamie's opinion.

There were plenty of dresses to fit her: dresses with flounces and furbelows, dresses of rustling pink silk and glistening white satin, glittering with pearls. There were blue velvet dresses and sophisticated crepe-de-chine dresses; plain dresses and fancy ones.

She would have none of them. "What's the fun of wearing a dress?" she asked. "I couldn't do anything for fear of soiling it. I have no dancing shoes, and there have been no balls so far aboard the ship. The gowns would be to no purpose. Please let me dress more simply."

Mrs. Llewellen sighed and raised her eyes to heaven, declaring that she would never permit any charge of hers to dress in any unsuitable manner.

But she did. Instead of a dress Amelia wore a bloused shirt, trousers (on a girl! thought Jamie), a kerchief, and low shoes.

A bloused shirt of gleaming white satin.

Trousers in the same material, but a brilliant scarlet.

Golden-glittery shoes.

A kerchief of silk, elaborately printed with green vines, yellow flowers, and red berries.

And to complete her ensemble, she found gold hoops to wear as earrings.

Jamie, getting his first look at her in this attire the morning after their rescue, said, "I hope Captain Hawke isn't following us. He could see that getup ten miles away."

Amelia laughed as if he had made the wittiest remark she had ever heard. She went about each day in that outfit, or another like it, looking like a pirate-girl out of a bad play. Jamie scolded her, but she only smiled at him. "You look like a boy," he finished, stalking off.

Yet he had to admit that she did not really look like a boy, not with her rich brown hair tumbling from beneath her kerchief, not with the grace of her movement and the sweetness of her face. When he caught himself thinking thus, Jamie snorted and took himself to a far corner of the ship.

At first everyone called Amelia "Princess," but she didn't like that and begged them all to call her by name. Soon it seemed natural just to call her "Amelia," or even "Amy." And try as he might to avoid her, Jamie found that Amelia was almost always underfoot. When she discovered that Jamie was having lessons, she asked to be allowed to share them.

"I'm not clever," she confided to Jamie the first morning they studied together at the table in the stern cabin. "In fact, I'm afraid I'm rather stupid. I expect it's hereditary. Mum says it comes from Da's side of the family. But maybe if I'm terribly confused you could help me?"

Jamie tried to look modest. "I'll try. Have you ever had lessons before?"

"Oh, yes. At home I had a mathematics tutor—he was the gardener too—and the cook taught me Zampish, and the upstairs maid—"

Jamie frowned. "I thought you were a princess. Didn't you have any tutors who were just tutors?"

Amelia bit her lip and shook her head. "Ours is a very poor kingdom," she said in a small voice. "Da was granted it after having served in some war or other years ago. He just called it the Kingdom of Two Mountains, a Valley, and Part of a Rather Small Lake, 'cos that's what was in it. You see, Da hasn't much imagination. But when he married Mum, she planted lots of bay trees and changed the name of the kingdom to Laurel."

"But you do have a palace and all?"

"Oh, yes! The most cunning little cottage you ever saw, red brick with the most darling trellis of climbing roses over the walkway to the front door. I have a room all to myself, and—"

"A cottage," Jamie said.

"Of course it's bigger than the servants' cottage next door, and it is on the fashionable side of Llaretun. That's the capital city, you know, and the only one in the whole kingdom. Would you like to know some of our history?"

"No," Jamie said.

As it happened, that morning's lessons had to do with history. Jamie told Amelia to let him answer any hard questions, since this was her first day.

Mr. Pye made his way down just on the dot of nine. "Well," he said, "we're on the open sea, we've a calm day, and so I may safely take an hour to instruct you young people."

He selected a large leather-bound volume from a shelf, found his place, and stood with the book balanced open on his right hand. He looked every inch the schoolmaster.

Mr. Pye cleared his throat. "I suppose, pedagogically speaking, I really should begin by determining how much you know. Let us consider the history of magic. Can either of your define the term 'Wizard King'?"

"That was Balmazor," Jamie said with confidence. "He had all sorts of great magic and could do more than a thousand spells—" he broke off, seeing Mr. Pye gently shake his head.

"You confuse fancy with fact, lad," the first mate said. "The thousand spells are a fable. Charming, to be sure, and most romantic, fit to be the subject of some fine poetry. I myself have—ah, but let it go, let it go." For a moment he stood with bowed head, looking more melancholy than ever. Then with a deep sigh, he said, "I suppose you are equally uninformed, Princess?"

"Well," Amelia said, blushing and biting her lip, "I'm not bright at history, but I *think* that Balmazor was a king who enlisted the aid of hundreds and hundreds of magicians who each had one talent, in the normal way. With their aid he united all of Anglavon as one kingdom, and he drove out the Voorish invaders, and he granted the West Countries independence in gratitude for their aid in the wars. And the chiefs there started to divide the land up into kingdoms, and so today the kingdoms have gotten really tiny, like my home kingdom of Laurel."

Jamie stared at her in complete astonishment.

"Excellent!" Mr. Pye said. "Listen to her well, Jamie."

And so it proved in all their lessons. Mr. Border might propound a difficult problem in applied mathematics: "A treasure galleon weighs anchor in New Madrid, setting sail for Zampia and heading eastward at ten knots. Meanwhile, out in the Gulf exactly one hundred sea-miles to the east a privateer of Anglavon (God save King Carleton!) shakes out canvas and sails west at twelve knots. We shall let line AB represent the intersecting courses of the galleon and the privateer. At what point C on the line AB shall the cowardly sons of Zampish rum-puncheons deliver up all their goods into the hands of the doughty privateers?"

Jamie would work furiously, but no matter how hard he tried, he was never first to say, "Point C is 45 1/2 sea-miles east of A and 54 1/2 sea-miles west of B."

It was almost too much to bear. Jamie studied hard, worked harder, and at last was able to correct Amelia when she faltered in translating a page of Classic Vrenkish, a triumph of which he continually reminded her for the next week.

Captain Deadmon vanished from sight after the first day, remaining in his sail locker. "The captain is self-conscious about his appearance," Pye confided to Mrs. Llewellen. "He prefers not to impose on you."

"Oh, la," Mrs. Llewellen returned. "Pray tell him that he will always live in my mind as our rescuer. As for looks, why he's quite a handsome corpse, most natural indeed."

Mr. Pye did not report, at least not in Jamie's hearing, how the captain reacted to these compliments, but his appearances on deck continued to be rare. In general the voyage went well, saving only those infrequent occasions when Barbecue Timson determined to assert his privileges and cook a meal.

But after the first occasion Mrs. Llewellen made it her business to be about the galley when Barbecue was cooking. Jamie suspected that her culinary expertise was something like Amelia's gift with lessons. The meals were still bad, but no one landed in sick bay after she began adding a pinch of this or a dash of that when Barbecue's back was turned.

In the intervals between lessons, Jamie continued to learn more about the ship and her management from the sailors. Of them all, Wicks was by far the friendliest. More than once Wicks, when standing lookout duty in the crow's nest, allowed Jamie to climb up and join him.

For his part, Jamie was often happy to avail himself of Wicks's courtesy, because Mrs. Llewellen refused to grant Amelia permission to climb the shrouds. There, high above the deck, he could be away from her for an hour or more.

"When will we see a ship of Anglavon?" Jamie asked Wicks on one of these expeditions.

"Ah, well, that's the question, isn't it?" Wicks responded, his gray eyes thoughtful. "Windrose Island's a tricksy kind o' place, ye see. Right smack on the Line she be, but the winds do blow so hard that it feels like the cold North Seas sometimes. And most ships avoid the region altogether, for the winds are never favorable there. We're a-crossing of some of the shipping lanes now, but the devil a friendly sail I've seen so far."

Wicks scanned the horizon. He reached into his pocket and produced a fat lemon—Deadmon had loaded whole barrels of them, since the fruit protected sailors from scurvy—which he halved with a new knife. "Want some?" he asked, holding out half the lemon to Jamie.

"No, thanks."

"Suit yourself." Wicks bit deeply and made a shivery gurgle. "Ah, sour!"

Jamie looked away, his mouth puckering. "Are dragons as bad as they say?" he asked.

"Ah, to be sure. They do say that dragons be fierce fighters. They breathes mostly fire, ye know. Some of 'em flies through the air on great bat wings, and some of 'em swims through the sea the same as serpents. But they all has great piles and heaps o' gold and jools, they say, and that's where they're the fiercest, for there's not a dragon as ever crawled that will suffer the loss o' his fortune without a fight."

"That's no place for a girl," Jamie said.

"That's as may be, lad." Wicks chuckled. "I believe that Mrs. Llewellen may prove a stout hand in a tight spot. Did ye see Mr. Pye's face when she shot the lock right off that musket? It was good as a play!"

Looking down at the deck, Jamie could just make out Mr. Pye standing not far from the foot of the mainmast. "What's wrong with Mr. Pye?" he asked Wicks. "He's so unhappy all the time. As if—as if there were something he regretted."

Wicks sucked the other half of the lemon loudly. "Ah," he said when he had finished. "Well, ye ain't far wide o' the mark there, Jamie, lad. There be men as goes to sea to forget some sorrow ashore, ye know. It may be that Mr. Pye is one o' them. But as for what has drove him to this life, well it'd be wrong o' me, as is merely a able-bodied sailor, to speculate."

"Sharkey says he would've stayed aboard the *Terror* to make sure that we got away."

"Oh, aye." Wicks's voice became gentle. "He's a good man, is Mr. Pye, and no doubt about that. But he does have some sorrow in his heart, and it's that keen that he takes little regard for his own life in a brawl."

Jamie sighed and took a deep breath of the bracing sea air. Six dolphins played at the bow, easily pacing the ship. Jamie scanned the horizon. "All clear, I see," he said.

Wicks gave him a quizzical look. "Well, aye, if ye disregards the Zampish craft, and the Tashkan one, and the Colonial brigantine, I suppose ye could say 'tis clear enough."

"What?"

"Look there, two points off to starboard," Wicks said.

Jamie peered in the direction of Wicks's pointing finger. Presently he said, "That *speck*?"

"Speck she may look, but she's a forty-four gun frigate, Tashkan by the cut of her sails, and a-heading for the South Colonies as fast as she may go. Now she'll drop her anchor in Brikola Harbor, like as not, and she'll come back laden with fruits and dyes and spices."

Wicks shifted and pointed off to the left. "Now look sharp for the triangle."

"I think I see it," Jamie said dubiously, for the spot on the horizon might have been triangular.

"Well, that's a Zampish sloop, bearin' south-sou'west. Headin' round Cape Storm, I warrant. Foes though they are, I wish the crew luck in them latitudes. And ye can't see her now, but there was a Colonial brigantine crossed our wake not many minutes ago."

"You must have some kind of seeing magic," Jamie said. "All I can make out are dots and specks."

Wicks looked pleased. "No, no magic. I was born without magic, as most people be, and I can't say's I ever wished it different. No offense to you, Jamie, but them few as has magic gets into about as much trouble with it as some sailors does with drink, and neither magic nor drink has much tempted me."

"Why do you think some people have magic and most don't?"

"Ask Mr. Pye. He's a deep thinker, and may have some reasons. Me, I think 'tis like having blue eyes, or a birthmark. 'Tis a plain accident of birth, and that's that."

Later, though, when Jamie asked Mr. Pye, the first mate's response, couched in philosophical terms, amounted to about as much as Wicks's uneducated opinion. The voyage progressed uneventfully.

Each morning and evening Mrs. Llewellen would promenade around the deck, accompanied by Mr. Pye. The crew, who quickly came to appreciate her efforts at improving Barbecue's execrable cookery, would tip her a cheery "Good morning, mum," or "Good evening," as the case might be. Amelia continued to apply herself to her lessons, and Jamie kept busy. Between lessons and duties, he had no time to admire the sea except at night and on Sabbath days.

Jamie always enjoyed the magical air of the ocean at night,

but on his last night watch he felt someone touch his hand and then clasp it. It was Amelia. "Let go," he said in irritation.

"Sorry," she said. "I'm frightened."

"Frightened?" Jamie asked, genuinely puzzled. "Of what?"

"It's so terribly dark," she said.

Jamie sighed elaborately. "There's nothing to be afraid of."

"Oh. Then I won't be."

"Who's there?" came a genial voice from the darkness.

Jamie recognized it as the third mate's voice. "It's only us, Mr. Caulker," he responded. "Jamie and Amelia."

"Ah." The mate joined them at the rail. He was smoking a pipe, and when he drew on it the tobacco in the bowl glowed brightly enough to show his bald head and the dark splotches of his wonderful tattoos. Caulker slept through the day, and Jamie and Amelia had seen little of him on the voyage.

"I was just saying we're safe because the *Betty*'s a sound ship," Jamie said.

"Aye, that she is," Caulker agreed. "I'd stake my life on the *Betty* long before I would on the newest ship of the line."

"I'm not worried now," Amelia said. "The crew seems awfully nice."

Caulker puffed his pipe. "Aye, worse luck. Times have changed, young people, times have changed. Why, I remember the days when Deadmon was man alive and master of the *Meteor*—for I've sailed along of him for thirty year and more, mind you—and when we hove into sight, why, often as not any ship in our path would strike her colors." Caulker laughed without much mirth. "Ah, 'tis a hard thing, but when a ship christened the *Bouncing Betty Bowers* heaves into view, nobody shakes in his boots."

"I think it's a lovely name," Amelia said.

"Oh, it'll do, lass, it'll do. See, 'twas the ship of old Cap'n Henery Bowers, the pirate, and we were sent after him when Bowers started plundering his majesty's ships. A most uxorious man was Henery Bowers—do you know that word?"

"Uxorious," Amelia said. "Greatly loving toward one's wife."

"Uh, yes," Jamie said.

"Right enough, right enough," Caulker agreed. "Well, he was married to a bonnie plump lady of Port Guldette, and he named his ship after her: The *Bouncing Betty Bowers* she was then, and that's what she is now. A craft fit to stand against any of that rascally Hawke's ships—or against a raging dragon."

Amelia stirred. "Oh, I want so badly to see a real live dragon."

Caulker chuckled. "Let's hope you don't see 'im too close, lass. It may be a death struggle—"

"Oh, no," Amelia said. "Poor dragon! I hope it doesn't come to that. Perhaps he may listen to reason."

"Uh—well, perhaps," Caulker muttered.

"Mr. Caulker," Jamie said, "I don't understand something. I've heard that no one's ever been to Windrose Island, and yet the captain has a map of the island. Who drew the map?"

Caulker knocked the ash from his pipe, and the red ember fell into the sea. "Well, 'tis a very old map, you understand. 'Twas done by Sir Edmond Drake's men about a hundred and fifty years ago. Drake, it seems, did find a passage to the island. His men came to the dragon's cavern, but for some reason nobody can understand, they never tried for the dragon's treasure. But one of the crew did the loveliest map you've ever seen, neat as you please—"

"A hundred and fifty years?" Amelia asked. "Isn't that rather a long time for a dragon to live?"

"Not particularly," Caulker said. "They can live to be two thousand. And it might have been a very young dragon."

"Has no one else found a way to the island?" Jamie asked.

"Not that we know of. Deadmon took the map from a Zampish captain. Not that it's done us any good, for the winds in them parts has always been dead against us." Caulker chuckled.

"What is it?" Amelia asked.

"Oh, I was just thinking, lass. 'Tis said that, oh, a hundred years ago, a captain named Morgan had possession of the map—

92

'twas he who lost it to the Zampians—and he made a bold attempt on the island. He commanded the fine old *Vengeance*.

"Well, even the *Vegeance* couldn't approach Windrose Island, for the contrary winds would drive her back every time. They say Morgan at last roared out, 'No fair wind! No fair wind! By the Powers, I'll *buy* myself a fair wind!' And with that he hurled a brass quartring into the sea.

"Now, the Powers o' the sea and sky don't take mockery lightly, and no sooner had that coin hit the waves than a hurricane sprang up. It bore the ship toward the island, but they missed it by a few rods. The howling gale was so strong that the ship had to run before it.

"Across the sea they flew, all the way to the Zampish Main, and at last the *Vengeance* fetched up with a horrible crash on the reefs near Holorita. A wreck she was, and the sailors dug into all that mess of timbers and ropes and spars and masts, and at the bottom lay old Morgan, a-cursing and a-raging. 'Captain:' someone said. 'Let this be a lesson: Ye can't buy wind.'

" 'Can't buy wind!' shouted old Morgan. 'I bought it, didn't I? But, by thunder! I wish afore I'd bought a whole quartring worth, I'd known it was so demnation cheap!' "

"Oh, the poor man," Amelia sighed. "And the Zampians captured him?"

"Aye, lass, but none of them was any luckier at reaching the island, and nobody today knows how old Drake might have managed it." Caulker stretched. "Well, I've got to make my rounds. My compliments, young folk!" He wandered away.

"Dragons," Amelia said in a dreamy kind of voice. "Oh, look. The moon's coming out."

During the voyage the moon had swelled to full, had shrunk to nothing, and had begun to wax again. Now it stood a day past first quarter, a silvery semicircle in the sky, a wrack of dark cloud scudding away to reveal it in its glory.

"It looks much lighter," Amelia said. "I'm not frightened at all now."

The blue moonlight sparkled on the waves. Jamie realized that Amelia was holding his hand again, but he was too tired of disengaging his fingers to let go. And besides, he thought, no one can see us here. No one can—

"Land ho!" shouted the lookout from the crow's nest. "Land ho, I say! Dead ahead, lads! 'Tis Windrose Island for certain!"

CHAPTER 9

Windrose Island

Practically the whole crew burst on deck, stretching and gabbling and pointing. Deadmon gave a curt order: "We'll stand off and try for a landing at dawn."

Men leaped into the shrouds and furled sail. Jamie badly wanted to climb to the crow's nest to get a better look at what was ahead of them, but this Mr. Pye absolutely refused to permit.

Still, the boy remained on deck after most of the sailors had gone below, for he felt a building excitement. He did rest on some coils of rope in the bow, and he must have slept a bit, for he had vivid dreams of great rearing dragons with fiery red eyes and huge gaping mouths with teeth like daggers, drooling red-hot spittle.

He thought of himself fighting a dragon, like the knights of the Wizard-King in the stories. But the likelihood of such combat was very small, and he felt relief at this fact. When the dragon had to be fought, the whole crew would do it. They would have at their command fourteen guns, enough—Jamie hoped—to pierce the hide of any old dragon.

At least Amelia had left him, for when Mrs. Llewellen found her on deck so late at night, the governess had fussed and scolded and had personally taken the princess below decks. But somehow or other Amelia got into Jamie's dragon dreams too. Girls had a way of spoiling everything.

When Jamie woke under a hot sun, he saw the captain, Mr.

Pye, and Mr. Border confabulating on the quarterdeck, and he hurried aft to listen to them. Tattersall, the youngish pilot, gripped the wheel in his lean hands. Stout Mr. Border held a large parchment map and was examining it closely.

"Hello, Jamie," Border said as the boy hurried toward them. "You look like the very devil. Too much excitement last night, I'll warrant."

"Is that the island?" Jamie asked, peering doubtfully at the map. It was a most peculiar looking island, something like an arrow shot through a squashed insect.

"Aye," said Deadmon. "The accursed landfall I've tried to make for thirty year and more. Where's the parrot?"

"Usually he stays in the galley. Shall I fetch him, sir?"

"If you please," Deadmon said, turning back to the map.

Jamie trotted forward. Squok liked the heat of the galley, and he roosted there on a pegged stand that the carpenter had knocked together for him. Jamie found the bird sound asleep, its head tucked under a wing. He poked Squok. "Come on. The captain wants you."

Squok woke and clacked his beak. "It's too early."

"Squok! Come on, please. Captain Deadmon will blame me if you don't."

Squok grumbled, but he hopped from his perch onto Jamie's shoulder. The boy hurried back to the men on the poop deck.

"Ah," said Deadmon as they came closer. "Here he is now. Well, Admiral Green, do you feel up for a flight this morning?"

Squok said, "Does it matter? I suppose I'll have to do it anyway. What's wanted?"

"Still the same blunt fellow," Pye said.

Deadmon merely nodded. "Admiral Green, if you look forward, you'll see some clouds on the horizon. Now, those clouds may or may not hide an island. We must know before we approach, so I'd like you to fly as high as you can and see what's under the clouds."

"Aye, aye, sir!" said Squok briskly, and he leaped into the air, flapping his wings. He circled the ship twice, then went spiraling up high in the sky.

"Excellent bird, that," Mr. Pye observed, shading his eyes as he followed Squok's ascent. "Most parrots are poor fliers, but Admiral Green has kept himself in wonderful condition."

Border, who noticed Jamie's interest in the map, held up the chart for him to look. "Now, lad, you see the island is really the root of this central mountain—a volcano, people say, but my opinion is that the smoke they occasionally glimpse is really from the dragon, who lives in a cavern here, where it says 'Dragon Hold'. There's one safe spot: Drake's Anchorage that spot is called, named for the only captain who's stopped there, and it lies in the natural harbor called 'The Nock'. To make this anchorage, we must swing 'round and come in from the south. If the map tells a true story, the anchorage is sheltered from the winds, and we can safely leave the ship there."

"But getting there," said Mr. Pye in his most pessimistic tone, "will be our great problem."

"Aye," said Mr. Tattersall, the pilot, from the helm. His features were as thin and sharp as Mr. Pye's, but where the first mate was a study in melancholy, Mr. Tattersall's face was a sketch of roguish humor. "Recall the time we dropped all sail and tried to tow her in with the boats?" Tattersall chuckled.

Mr. Border said without looking up, "We had bad luck on that occasion, that's all."

Mr. Tattersall laughed as if all bad luck in the world were a delightful joke. "Aye, that's the point. It might have worked if we'd had the luck to see the blessed island before breaking out the oars. But we didn't, did we? The wind blasted us away, and didn't you lads have a wet time of it trying to scramble aboard before they turned turtle, though?"

Shivering, Border shook his head at the memory. "A near thing, and some of us sick for weeks after. Well, now we have our wind-changer with us, and so we may hope for better success." He put his blunt forefinger back on the map. "Anyway, lad, I was telling you that we'll try to drop anchor here, in the Nock. From there we'll take the boats as far north up this crooked river as we can. That's Corkscrew Stream." His finger moved northward on the parchment. "And at last we go overland to the foot of the smoking mountain here. After that, it's a climb to Dragon Hold, and may all the Powers help us then."

Jamie looked away over the starboard rail. The bank of cloud was off ahead of them still, a few points north of west. Captain Deadmon said, "Do you know a song to call a good wind up from the south, lad?"

Jamie mused. "Well, there's 'Sweet Southern Wind,' but that's a lullaby and just calls up breezes. Then there's 'The Way of the Wind,' but that's got southeastern and western winds in it too, and I generally get whirlwinds and gusts with that one. The best one might be 'South Wind Blow Me Home,' because that calls up a good southern wind to take a sailor home."

"The very thing," Border declared. "It's—"

He broke off as Squok came spiraling down. The parrot came to rest on Deadmon's shoulder, where he perched panting loudly. "Pinfeathers, but that was a flight," he gasped.

"Well, Admiral Green? What did you see?" Deadmon asked.

"It's the island, Cap'n, that's for sure," Squok said. "But you've got hours to sail before you can see land from deck."

"My thanks to you, Admiral Green. Mr. Tattersall, the ship is yours. Mr. Border, show him our approach. Now look lively, all, for this may be our only chance to plunder the hoard of a living dragon. Fall to, my hearties, fall to!"

Jamie thought that for the first time since he had known the captain there was something like expression in the hollow voice. Deadmon sounded as enthusiastic as anyone could reasonably expect a corpse to be.

Not long after the ship began the wide, circling course that would permit them to approach the island from the south, Princess Amelia came on deck, dressed in her usual gaudy colors: a yellow shirt this morning, with a green and yellow sash at the waist, and bright green trousers. "It's warm already," was her mild observation.

Indeed it was, for the ship was almost exactly on the equator, and in the sultry heat of that latitude the winds were local and tricky. Both Amelia and Jamie had to find a spot out of the way of the sailors, and they met at the stern rail. "What are they doing?" Amelia asked.

Jamie scowled, but he did not really mind taking the opportunity to tell Amelia of the island and of their means of approach. She listened with interest, nodding to show that she understood. Meanwhile men in the rigging and on deck trimmed the sails to Mr. Tattersall's orders, and the ship obediently made headway in a great arc to the west and the south.

Gradually the bank of cloud slipped off to starboard, then around toward the stern. As the sun rose, the clouds became shining white on top, but even at a great distance Jamie could see the dark gray undersides, shadowed and looking full of wind and thunder.

Wicks was on deck, working with the other sailors. At one point he put his hand beside his mouth and shouted up to another sailor, a tall blond fellow named Jorgen, who occupied the crow's nest: "Look alive, there, mate! What's behind us?"

The lookout's voice came down thinned by distance: "Clouds, I suppose, but I don't like the looks of little black specks on the aft horizon, that's for sure." Jamie looked astern and glimpsed a tiny dark shadow afar off.

Finally, past noon, Mr. Pye clapped Jamie on the shoulder. "We're close enough, lad. Time to whistle!"

Hardly enough breeze stirred to move a sail or flutter a pennant, and the heat weighed heavy on all of them. Even Mrs. Llewellen, who was always cool, looked wilted, though she had put by her sober black widow's dresses for a white cotton one, very simple and somehow making her look years younger. She and Amelia stood together in the stern.

Strutting a bit with self-importance, Jamie joined the captain beside the wheel, where Mr. Tattersall, his white shirt translucent from sweat, gave him a weary smile. Of them all, only Deadmon, dressed as always in his captain's coat and tricornered hat, looked cool; but then, Jamie reflected, he had a good reason to look so.

"We are directly south of the inlet now," Deadmon said. "With a good following wind, we should make the anchorage an hour before sunset. It's up to you, lad. Whistle us up a wind—a wind for the dragon's lair."

Wicks, who was standing on one of the mizzen yards overhead, caught up the cry: "Hurrah! A wind for the dragon's lair!" And the other crewmen took it up too, raising a hearty, though weary, cheer that thrilled Jamie and almost made him feel cold, even in that great heat.

"Aye, aye, sir," he said. He licked his lips, took a deep breath, and began the song called "South Wind Blow Me Home":

'Twas years and years I left my girl,
And sailed away to sea;
'Tis years and years I've roamed the world,
  And no sweet love for me;
  But my heart seeks harbor now;
I want no more to roam,
So blow softly from the south, ye wind,
  Oh, south wind, blow me home!

Slowly, reluctantly, as if it too had been made stupid and sluggish by the heat, the wind began to stir. The scarlet pennant at the foretop squirmed like an eel, made a halfhearted flap or two, and at last began to flutter. The sails filled with air as the ship got under way.

Jamie whistled harder, all the way to the end of the song, and then grinned as another round of cheers went up for him. "Will that hold, do you think?" Deadmon asked him anxiously.

"Aye, aye, Captain," Jamie replied. "I whistled hard. It should be good for the rest of the day.

"Mr. Tattersall?" Deadmon asked.

The pilot grinned. "A good easy eight knots, sir, and near six hours o' daylight left. I calculate landfall well before sunset at this rate."

Someone touched Jamie's shoulder. It was Amelia, her brown

eyes worshipful. "You whistled very well," she said. "The sailors at home sing that song too."

"Oh," Jamie replied carelessly, "it was nothing. I didn't know that Laurel was a seaside kingdom."

"Oh, yes," Amelia said eagerly. "Our capital is a seaport, you know, at the mouth of a darling little river. We have a good harbor and export leeks, potatoes—"

"I wonder how big the dragon is," Jamie said.

Amelia bit her lip. "How big do they grow?"

"All sizes," screeched a high voice. Squok came swooping down to Jamie's shoulder. "Some no bigger than sparrows. Those are little gray dragons, confined to certain areas of the Hindi ocean."

"A dragon the size of a bird?" Amelia asked wonderingly.

"Aye, aye," Squok said, looking wise. "But they don't gather hoards like their bigger cousins. Instead, they simply hunt for insects in the brush and kill them with little jets of flame. We collected some as curiosities once, and the captain made a good business selling them as fire starters. But other dragons are huge. Some are the size of mountains, they say, and they fish in the sea for right whales, which they eat six at a bite, like Mr. Border snacking on sardines."

"Oh," Amelia said.

The thought made Jamie uneasy, and he wandered off to find the first mate. "Well, lad," Pye said with his sorrowful smile, "you've done it. Before long we'll see the island ahead."

"Sir," Jamie said, "excuse me, but how do we fight a dragon?"

"Frightened, are you?" Pye asked, giving Jamie a keen look.

"Oh, no, not at all," Jamie protested, but his throat was tight and the words came out high-pitched.

"No shame if you are, for a dragon's a frightful thing for anyone to face. If there's a man aboard who is *not* frightened, he's not the kind of sailor I'd want for a shipmate."

"Are you frightened, sir?"

Pye heaved a sigh and looked away. "Ah, well, I'm a special case, you see. The captain is not afraid because his body is dead, and I am not afraid because—never mind. Suffice it to say that some of us have seen the worst life has to offer. After that, no threat can make us shiver. No, lad, I am not myself frightened, but that does not mean I am brave."

Jamie reached to hold onto a stay. "I don't understand. Not to be afraid—that's courage, isn't it?"

"No," Pye said softly. "To be afraid and yet to do one's duty regardless of fear; to feel stark terror and then to put it behind one; to shake and shiver at certain death and yet keep oneself clearheaded to think and strong-willed to act—these are courage. To face danger and not to be afraid is not bravery, lad, but idiocy. So be afraid, but master your fear."

Mr. Tattersall suddenly yelled for Jamie, and he hurried back to the wheel, leaving Mr. Pye brooding in the bows.

"Yes, sir?" Jamie asked the pilot.

"Can't ye smell it?" Tattersall asked. "Take a deep breath, boy, can't ye smell it?"

Jamie inhaled. The smells were those he had become accustomed to: salt air, old wood heated by the sun, tar, sweat, and—and something more. Something that smelled green and growing. It was—"Land!" Jamie cried.

"Aye," Tattersall said. "And that's all wrong. For if the wind you whistled be constant, then it's blowing toward the only land in these waters. We shouldn't be able to smell it at all. Your wind is dying, lad."

"Land!" cried the lookout from above. "Land ho! 'Tis a great sharp peak of a mountain, dead ahead! Land ho! 'Tis Windrose Island, for certain sure—"

And in the next instant his voice was utterly lost as a hurricane blasted the ship.

CHAPTER 10

Whistling Up the Wind

The blast of wind brought Captain Deadmon to the wheel, booming orders: "Aloft! Reef the mainsail! Lively, lively!"

The waves had become mountainous, streaked with white foam. The ship sped away from the island in the shadow of a shelf of dark cloud, yet to either side sunlight sparkled on the waves.

Tattersall fought the wheel. Spray drenched Jamie. "Shall I whistle?" he cried out over the screaming wind.

"Nay!" Tattersall bellowed. "For you might call up a contrary wind that'd put us in a whirlabout."

Deadmon had come up close. "The wind will fall off soon. 'Tis ever thus with Windrose Island. We come close enough to see land, and then the wind turns against us and rushes us off."

Mr. Pye came panting up, his curly graying hair plastered to his forehead. "No damage done, Captain. All hands safe."

"And the women?"

"Gone below, sir, though I think Clara could stand toe by toe with our sailors and work the ship, she's that fine a lass."

Clara? Jamie puzzled over that one for a moment before realizing that Clara must be Mrs. Llewellen's christened name. "Where's Squok?" he asked Mr. Pye.

"Below with the ladies. He was in the rigging, and the wind tumbled him from the mizzen to the foremast. He lost some tail-feathers, but he's well."

"And, uh, Amy—I mean the princess?"

Pye glanced at Jamie. "You might just nip down to my cabin and check on her."

"Aye, sir," said Jamie.

"And return here when the wind's eased," Deadmon ordered. "You'll have to whistle again."

The stormy waves made Jamie reel his way below deck. He tapped at the door of Mr. Pye's old cabin, and it opened a crack. Mrs. Llewellen's bright blue eye peered out at him.

"Yes, Jamie?"

"Uh—Mr. Pye thought I might see if you—if the princess and you—and I was worried about the parrot—"

"Come in."

Three were a crowd in the small cabin. Amelia had changed to more sensible clothes: a homespun sailor's blouse and trousers. A bedraggled Squok perched on the back of her chair. "Well," the bird said. "And what happened to your wind, you wonder-worker?"

"Now, now," Amelia murmured. "Jamie did his best."

Jamie murmured, "Do you, uh, need anything?"

"No, thank you," Amelia said gravely. "Are we sinking?"

"Sinking!" Jamie exclaimed. "The *Betty?* Never. But I'll have to whistle another wind as soon as we turn the ship."

"Why didn't the first wind last longer?" Amelia asked.

Jamie shrugged miserably. "I don't know. Perhaps the dragon's magic overpowers mine. Maybe the words are too weak."

"The words?" asked Mrs. Llewellen.

"Aye—I mean, yes, ma'am. I have to have the words in my head when I whistle a tune. Some songs have strong words—'The Cold Nor'easter,' for instance, with its lines about 'the howling gale' and 'the killing wind.' Other songs have weak words, and 'South Wind Blow Me Home' is one of those."

Mrs. Llewellen put a forefinger on her chin. "Stronger words mean stronger wind?"

"Yes, but I don't know any. I shall have to try to whistle harder and louder," Jamie said.

Squok made a derisive sound.

Jamie left the ladies in the cabin and made his way topside again. The wind had abated to a stiff gale, and Mr. Tattersall brought the *Betty*'s head around into it.

"I'm ready to try again, sir," Jamie reported to Deadmon.

The captain looked to Mr. Tattersall. The pilot nodded. "Aye, sir. Let the lad try. 'Twill be hard getting her in before nightfall, but we ought to make the attempt."

"Very well, lad," Deadmon said. "Whistle us a wind."

Jamie pursed his lips and began the same song as before. Presently the headwind died down and a following wind sprang up, though not nearly as strong as the blast that had forced them back. "Look at that," Mr. Pye said, pointing to port.

Jamie glanced aside. Twenty yards to the left the wind was still blowing southward, out from Windrose Island. Then the north-trending wind that Jamie had whistled up began. Spumes of spray and miniature waterspouts marked the meeting of the winds.

By now the whole sky was uniformly overcast and gray, though the temperature remained sultry. Jamie sweated as he whistled the same tune, monotonously, over and over. The ship made a league, then two. Finally Wicks, who had replaced Jorgen up in the crow's nest, sang out, "Land ho! Windrose Island again!"

Jamie whistled as if his life depended on it. His jaw began to ache, his tongue to cramp. "How far away?" Deadmon cried.

"Four leagues," hazarded Wicks.

"Two hours," grunted Tattersall. "We'll make it by dark."

Mr. Pye looked hard at Jamie. "Are you tiring, Jamie, boy?"

Jamie nodded wearily.

Deadmon laid a heavy hand on his shoulder. "Can you keep it up for another two hours?"

Jamie's heart misgave him.

"Jamie," Mr. Pye said, "if you feel yourself unable to continue, tug my sleeve. Give us time to take in sail and so prevent our being dashed away from the island."

Jamie nodded and went on whistling.

But two hours was an optimistic estimate. Before fifteen minutes had passed, Mr. Tattersall reported, "Wind's falling off." And after another fifteen minutes, he sighed, "Dead calm."

"Reef the sails," Deadmon ordered.

Jamie's notes faltered, but somehow he kept up the tune until the *Betty* lay under almost bare poles. Then Deadmon said, "Ease off, lad, and let's see what happens."

Jamie stopped gratefully, his lips sore from puckering. At once the wind reversed itself and became again that raging hurricane. But this time the *Betty* had battened down for it, and the ship did not suffer as badly, though the men fought just to hold her position.

Jamie retired to his berth and lay there wrapped in a cocoon of self-pity as the porthole darkened with the coming of night. At last someone knocked. "Come in," Jamie said listlessly.

The door slid open. It was Amelia. "What's wrong?"

Jamie rolled away from her and lay staring at the bulkhead. "I failed. I can't hold the wind."

"Oh," Amelia said.

"I'm sorry you're taking it so badly," Jamie said. "I can tell that it just breaks your heart."

"I didn't say—"

Jamie wouldn't let her continue: "Or maybe you don't even care. Of course girls have other things to worry about, like their clothes and their hair—"

"I'm not worrying about those things," she said, sounding a little hurt.

Jamie felt a twinge of regret at his sarcasm, but something inside wouldn't let him stop. He said, "And you're a princess too. You're probably worried about your father and mother, the king and queen, sitting on those hard thrones all day—"

Amelia actually laughed. "Mum and Da don't have *thrones.* Mum has a comfy chair with roses on it, but Da generally holds court with his old army chums all sitting around the kitchen table. It's more friendly-like, he says, and it's closer to the cellar if he wants a pint or so now and again—"

"Please," Jamie said, "just leave me alone."

"I'm sorry." Amelia bit her lip. "I know I'm dreadfully ignorant and chattery. Only—didn't you get tired, whistling all that time? I know I would have."

"Yes," Jamie said. "I think it would be good to give my lips a rest now. All by myself."

"I'm afraid you can't. You see, Mr. Pye sent me down to fetch you."

"What! Why didn't you—" Jamie swung out of the bunk.

Amelia flattened her back against the corridor wall and Jamie squeezed past her.

"Here he is," Mr. Pye said as Jamie came on deck. "Lad, it's getting dark, we've lost way, and, in short, it's time for you to whistle again. To it, Jamie, and with all your might!"

Jamie tried, but nothing happened. He could not properly pucker his lips. A rush of air came out, but no tune.

Mr. Tattersall, looking bone-weary, said, "If we can't get a wind soon, sir, we'll fall away. Tomorrow we'll be no closer to the island, with no better hopes of getting there."

"Try, lad," Mr. Pye urged.

Jamie blew until his cheeks puffed out, but he got only a reedy note or two, not even enough to stir a breeze. Mrs. Llewellen came on deck with Amelia. They stood quietly watching him as he felt his face turning red with effort.

"No luck," Mr. Pye said.

The captain turned away and gave a groan. The deep sadness of it made Jamie blink, and he could not help feeling to blame. He stopped trying to whistle, tears stinging in his eyes.

"Here," Amelia said, coming close and holding out her hand. "See if this will help."

She held out half a lemon.

Jamie swallowed, looked at her—she smiled sweetly and with no hint of rebuke—and took the lemon. Mr. Pye, Mr. Tattersall, and Mrs. Llewellen all held their breaths. Jamie bit into the sour fruit, felt the acid gush of its juice over his tongue. His lips automatically puckered. He tried to whistle—

107

And the first notes of "South Wind Blow Me Home" came out clear and sharp. A fitful south wind stirred, and the ship moved ever so gently.

Deadmon roared, "Break out more sail, my lads! This may be our last chance!"

Again sailors rushed up and down the masts and all over the deck. The *Betty* picked up some speed, though not much, as the wind rose. She moved forward yard by agonizing yard, until Jamie's song and the magic wind from the island reached a stand-off. Jamie whistled, but the ship lay in a dead calm. By now heavy twilight had settled, and they faced a long night with no hope of landfall.

Deadmon ordered the sails reefed again, and again Jamie stopped whistling and the contrary island wind sprang up. This time, though, they were a bit closer to the island, and they did not seem to fall away so fast.

"I'm sorry, sir," Jamie muttered, and his voice sounded rusty even to himself. "If only I knew a better song—"

Mrs. Llewellen came up behind Jamie and put her hands on his shoulders. "Captain, Jamie can whistle a stronger wind if he knows stronger words. There is one man aboard who can give him those words."

Deadmon stared at her for a long moment, then turned away. "Madam, I cannot ask—"

"Mr. Pye," said Mrs. Llewellen so softly that Jamie could hardly hear her, "will you write lyrics for a song if I provide the tune?"

The first mate looked thunderstruck. For a moment he said nothing. He finally stammered, "Madam, I—I hardly—"

"You," she said, "are a poet."

Captain Deadmon moaned, and Mr. Tattersall said, "Uh-oh. Now she's done it."

Mr. Pye's face flamed red in the light of the stern lanterns. "Madam," he said with cold fury, "you are mistaken."

Mrs. Llewellen lifted her head high, and the wind made her hair trail out like a comet's tail. "No, sir, I am not. For, you see, in the cabin you lent us I discovered your manuscripts, and I have read them. Oh, sir, you are indeed a poet."

Mr. Pye averted his face. "Nay, madam. I once aspired to be a poet—but that is long past." He took a deep breath, broken by an almost silent sob. "It is true that when I was a mere lad of nineteen, newly arrived at college, I scribbled some foolish verses and had the gall to have them privately printed. Alas, the reaction of the critics swept from my mind all notion of being a poet. They called me an enthusiast, a dilettante, a barbaric voice crying in the flush of youth. They said I lacked that regularity of mind, that fine sense of proportion, that a poet needs."

"Then," said Mrs. Llewellen, "the critics were mistaken, that's all. Dear Mr. Pye, I have read your works: 'Ode to Solitude'; 'A Salute to the Morning'; 'The Lonely Star.' These are poems, Mr. Pye, written by a true poet."

Deadmon almost looked interested. "She's right, my boy," he rumbled. "It's as I've always said: you are not a neoclassic poet, but you are a fine romantic poet. The pity of it is that you were born out of your time. But what of that? It merely means that you shall have to wait a hundred years after your death before some grubbing student of literature discovers your poetry. Then you will be as celebrated as any of that scribbling tribe, depend upon it!"

Jamie touched Mr. Pye's arm. "Please, sir," he said humbly. "I don't know anything about poets or poetry. But I do know that I need help. Indeed, we all do."

Mr. Pye stood irresolute. In a voice shaking with emotion, he said, "Boy, you do not know what you ask. My heart has been rent, my very soul has been torn, by critics."

Jamie staggered as the headwind made the ship pitch. "Sir, be afraid of the critics if you wish, but be brave and write the words, I beg you."

Mr. Pye walked across the unsteady deck, stood with his back to them for a moment, and finally turned. "The boy puts me to shame. Very well, madam. Let us repair to the stern cabin. What do you require?"

She said, "I cannot write music, but I can play any tune that comes to mind. I don't suppose there is such a thing as a harpsichord aboard?"

"Aye, madam," said Deadmon. "For we plundered an enemy ship two years ago, and some of the sailors fetched off a fine harpsichord, thinking it a fancy musical treasure chest. I'll have it moved aft. Hurry, both of you! For some fate is on me now, and somehow I am certain that tonight we must attempt the landing or fail forever."

"Aye, aye, sir!" said Mr. Pye, snapping the captain a formal salute. He offered his arm to Mrs. Llewellen. "Clara."

"Why thank you—Andrew."

The next hour was the worst of Jamie's life. When the ship fell off too much, he whistled a few bars of his song, just enough to touch them back on the right heading, for he knew he had to save his strength. The ship rolled and pitched as night fell. Mr. Tattersall went off duty to snatch a meal and a few minutes of rest before their next attempt. Big Ned Sharkey took the wheel in his stead, and it looked small in his hands.

Jamie confessed his misery to Amelia, who listened with solemn interest. At last she said, "You did your best."

"But the wind always stayed constant before," he groaned. "For a day or two, anyway. And now my head's beginning to hurt."

"Well," Amelia said reasonably, "you never had to fight another magic wind before, that's all."

The headwind grew more boisterous. At last Mr. Pye sent for Jamie. He entered the rolling stern cabin to find Mr. Pye leaning on an elaborately carved and decorated harpsichord which took up almost all the floor space in the cramped cabin. A demure Mrs. Llewellen sat at the keyboard. "Listen, Jamie," said Mr. Pye. "Play, Clara."

With a smile, Mrs. Llewellen performed a jigging tune, lively and catchy. Jamie had it by heart the first time he heard it. "Now," Pye said. "The tune is Cla—Mrs. Llewellen's. Alas, the words are my own. Get them by rote, and may the poor things bring you more luck than they have brought me."

"He is modest," said Mrs. Llewellen. "It's a fine poem."

110

Blushing, Mr. Pye cleared his throat and read from a paper besmirched by many crossed-out lines and false starts:

O southern wind, rise strong and true;
Not as a babe's breath, mild and soft,
But as though some mad god aloft
In his fury commanded you!

Rise, rise, and rage, as you oft
In stories old did rage and rave;
Be master of both cloud and wave,
Until night has its black cloak doffed.

O wind, be master and no slave!
Great southern gale, arise today;
Be strong, be swift, and keep your way
While yet I sing to thee my stave.

He ceased reading, coughed, and went bright red. "I regret the inversion in line eight. I got myself into a bit of trouble with the rhyme—"

"There," said Mrs. Llewellen. "It's lovely. Jamie?"

"Say the words again," he said.

Mr. Pye recited the lyric twice more. At Mrs. Llewellen's suggestion, Jamie sang the song. "Oh, Jamie," said Amelia—who had followed him without his even realizing it—"what a sweet voice you have." Jamie almost choked.

"You have it," said Mrs. Llewellen, standing up. "Now let's try it!"

The four of them hurried back on deck. Mr. Tattersall had resumed his post at the wheel, looking remarkably fresh and rested after barely an hour away from the helm. Deadmon, his face more corpselike than ever in the glare of the lanterns, said, "Well?"

"We are ready to try, sir," said Mr. Pye.

Deadmon raised his hat. "Madam," he said, "you have done something that I have not been able to do for thirty years: You've made Andrew Pye admit that he is indeed a poet. He needs you, madam, and I would take it as a personal kindness if, when this voyage ends, you would marry him."

"Oh, la," said Mrs. Llewellen. "I'd be delighted to."

Mr. Pye grinned very foolishly, but he said nothing.

"Now, lad," said Deadmon, clapping his hat back on his head, "Whistle!"

Amelia, standing beside Jamie, leaned forward and kissed him on the cheek. "For luck," she whispered, and she pressed half a lemon into his hand.

Jamie took a deep breath, heard the song in his head, remembered the words, and whistled. The tune came out brilliantly, and Mr. Tattersall began to sway to its rhythm as he steered. The sailors seemed to climb into the shrouds to the same beat, and even the captain's dead toe began to tap.

This time the hurricane sprang up from behind, shouting like a thousand waterfalls and sending the ship true as an arrow on a northward course.

CHAPTER 11

In the Dragon's Lair

So potent was the new song that Jamie had to whistle it only twice. The ship boomed along with all sails filled, and Mr. Tattersall steered with wonderful sureness. He had Mr. Border hold the chart up, and Wicks illuminated it with a shaded lantern, and then with only an occasional glimpse at the chart, Tattersall adjusted the wheel minutely and exactly.

Mr. Pye stood beaming. When Mrs. Llewellen came close to him, he slyly slipped his arm around her waist.

Gradually Jamie became aware of a growing tension in Mr. Tattersall's attitude, an air of expectancy. "Stand by to lower sail," he said, and Mr. Pye shouted the order at the top of his lungs. The men scurried into the rigging.

"Now!" Mr. Tattersall yelled. The sails dropped as if bewitched. "Drop the anchor!" Iron plummeted from the bows.

The ship rocked lazily. With a flourish Mr. Tattersall relinquished the wheel and saluted the captain. "Drake's Anchorage, sir."

"A course well-enchanted, Mr. Tattersall." Deadmon turned away. "Mr. Pye," he said in a low voice, "pray order the lamps extinguished."

As soon as the lamps were out, Jamie could see the dark bulk of land on both sides of the ship. "Windrose Island," Deadmon said. "At last!"

A great cheer went up, and Jamie found that Amelia was holding his hand. In the darkness he did not mind as much, and he squeezed her fingers a little.

"Captain," said Mr. Pye, "what are your orders?"

"Why," Deadmon said, "let's go ashore, for unless I'm much mistaken, not a man of the crew will sleep at all tonight, not with the end of our journey so near." He turned to Mr. Tattersall. "Pilot, will the *Betty* ride safely here?"

"Like a babe in her cradle, sir," Tattersall said. "The Nock is a well-protected harbor."

"Captain," Mr. Pye said, "I would feel uneasy leaving the *Betty* quite unmanned. Then too, we have our passengers to consider."

Deadmon nodded. "You're always right, Mr. Pye. The women may remain aboard. Who will volunteer to guard the ship?"

The query flashed through the crew, and in the end three men stepped forward: Sailors named Stefendor, Megalister, and Aupont agreed to stand watch on the *Betty*, the first because he had a severe cold, the second because he did not believe in dragons and did not wish his prejudices altered, and the last because he was not gregarious and would relish solitude for a while.

Deadmon appointed them guards, and then ordered, "Everyone else, man the boats. Mr. Pye, you will command the new pinnace. I will take the longboat, Mr. Tallow will command the jolly boat, and Mr. Caulker will have the gig. We shall row up the Corkscrew Stream, establish a camp, and at dawn we shall try this dragon's mettle."

Again the men cheered. Mr. Border and two others opened the arms locker and distributed pistols and cutlasses. When Jamie's turn came—of course he had hurried to get in line—Mr. Border merely shook his head. "Sorry, lad. Cabin boys aren't armed as a usual thing, you know. Next!"

Jamie immediately remembered the brace of pistols he had seen in the great cabin, and in a trice he found them and thrust them into his belt, under his shirt. Then, feeling armed to the teeth, he went back on deck, where the mates overseeing the boats assigned each man a place. Jamie was to go in the pinnace with the captain. His enthusiasm was only slightly dampened when Barbecue Timson asked his help in lowering a bulky crate into the boat. "Cookery things," he confided. "For 'tis only fitting that for our first night on shore I prepare a feast for the men."

Jamie debated whether or not he should accidentally drop the crate into the bay. Sober reflection persuaded him that Timson would only prepare another one, and so with the air of a martyr Jamie helped the cook safely stow his cargo.

The gig led the way up the twisting river, a lantern in its prow illuminating the way. The larger boats followed, with the pinnace second in line. Her bows carried powerful lanterns, aimed at the banks, which were steep in most places, pitted gray rock spangled and festooned with green lianas, flowering vines, and fleshy white orchids.

Once they passed a flat beach of black sand, occupied by shoals of huge olive green reptiles lying on their bellies. "Dragons?" whispered a sailor when they saw the creatures.

"Crocodiles," Deadmon said shortly.

They passed on, the oarsmen working against a sluggish current, until the wind began to buffet them, coming from directly ahead. "We've passed the bluffs," Deadmon said. "Now the thing to do is to find a landing place, and off to port yonder I think I spy a very good one."

The people in the gig thought so too, evidently, for the bobbing lantern at her prow turned left and eventually stopped. Jamie saw the light obscured several times as sailors leaped out and hauled the gig up onto the beach.

The other boats followed. Jamie helped his shipmates out, leaning against the wind, and together they made their way up the beach to a spot where Deadmon joined the crew of the gig. "The very place. Set up camp, lads."

Jamie tried to help gather wood, but his legs were unsteady. For more than a month he had accustomed himself to walking the rolling deck of a ship, and now he staggered as the land obstinately refused to roll. Another sailor, a slight figure in the dark, seemed to be having the same trouble. Jamie steadied him, and the sailor squeezed his hand.

"You!"

"Of course," Amelia said.

"But you were to stay aboard! Captain Deadmon said—"

"Said we *may* remain aboard. I didn't wish to."

Jamie scowled into the darkness. "Did you ask Mrs. Llewellen for permission to come?"

"Of course not, silly. She'd just refuse. Now help me learn how to walk again." Jamie, not knowing what else to do, helped her until, with practice, both of them adjusted their gaits to solid land. Halfway through their promenade they suddenly came upon the tall, slender silhouette of Mr. Pye. "Jamie," he said. "Who's that with you?"

"Me, Mr. Pye," Amelia said in a cheerful voice. "However do you manage to walk so well both on land and on the ship?"

"You," Pye said. "I'm dashed."

"Oh, don't be cross. I've never seen a dragon before."

Mr. Pye sighed. "I suppose it's no good scolding you. Very well, I shall have a small tent set up just for you, young lady. But I hope you realize that Clara will be worried about you."

"I think not," she said. "All the sailors who stayed behind to mind the ship are ombre players, and that's her favorite card game. She probably will not even miss me."

Mr. Pye went away shaking his head.

The sailors had chosen as a campsite a level space protected by a semicircle of huge boulders, and here a cheerful bonfire already burned. One of the sailors showed Amelia her tent. She pronounced it darling and immediately set about gathering leaves for a mattress and flowers to decorate her bedroom, as she was pleased to call it. Jamie went searching for Mr. Pye.

The boy found the first mate and Mr. Border bending over the map, holding it so as to catch the blazing light of the fire. "We are here," said Mr. Border, his blunt finger marking a spot halfway up the peninsula that ended in the Nock. "And tomorrow we shall have to march to the base of the mountain."

"Two hours," said Mr. Pye.

"No more," agreed Mr. Border.

"And then the assault on the dragon," said a familiar hollow voice. Captain Deadmon stepped forward with Squok on his shoulder. "And if the Powers smile on us, by sunset tomorrow you will all be rich men. And I—I shall be free." His voice quavered with such unaccustomed emotion that Jamie could not bear it. He walked away from the men and stood in the darkness for a while, all by himself.

Then, with a flurry of wings, Squok came to sit on his shoulder. "The captain is proud of you," said the parrot.

Jamie nodded. "I hope he has reason to be. Do you suppose there's really a dragon?"

Squok shifted his weight. "Who knows? For the captain's sake, I hope there is—and that it's a small one."

"And if there is, then Captain Deadmon will be released from his curse, and he'll—he will go away. I'll find that hard."

Squok sighed. "We all will. But it's time and past time that Captain Deadmon went to his long rest. And maybe his spirit will be happier sailing those unknown waters, after all."

Jamie hoped Squok was right, but it was a sorrowful notion to think on, and even after he lay down in one of the tents, the prospect of losing the captain's company made him sad. Somehow or other, toward midnight, he fell asleep at last. He dreamed of the old Pirate's Rest. It seemed to him that the pirate on the sign came to life and climbed down, proclaiming that he must be off on his business, and that Mr. Growdy, displeased, pinched Jamie's ears unmercifully in retaliation.

So vivid was the dream that when Jamie awoke next morning, he found that his ear actually ached. So did his stomach, for in the dark he had managed to avoid Barbecue's banquet. Now he leaped to his feet with a keen appetite.

Jamie climbed to the top of one of the boulders, where the

wind buffeted him, though not as strongly as it had in the night. He leaned into it and looked about with wonder. On either side of him grew thick forest, with the river cutting through it off to his right. It was the oddest forest he had ever seen, for it grew sideways. Trees grew straight for two or three feet, but then they began to curve, until their trunks were parallel to the ground, pointing outward from the center of the island.

The wind, Jamie realized, had shaped the trees. He slipped down from the rock, found Amelia, who had already breakfasted, and took her to see the view. She was properly awed, though she worried more about Jamie's empty stomach than about seeing the landscape. He indulged her and went back to the campfire, where he ate enough fried ham and biscuits to reassure her.

Deadmon, Pye, and Border took the lead as they broke camp and marched toward the central mountain of the island, an imposing pinnacle of dark gray rock. Just as they got underway, Jamie heard the sound of a distant explosion, like muffled thunder, but none of the others seemed to notice it, and after a moment he concluded that the wind had played a trick with his hearing. He fell in beside Amelia and said nothing.

The wind lost strength as they proceeded northward, and the trees gradually grew straighter, until at last they walked in the deep shade of a regular forest. Eons of leaf mould lay springy beneath their feet and little brown birds chirped and fluttered away from their path in sudden alarm. The march might have taken two hours, but to Jamie it seemed only minutes before they saw before them the very pinnacle sketched on the map.

It rose like a funnel set upside down. For the first third of its height, its slope was not great; for the next third it was formidable; and for the top third it was sheer. And just at the end of the gentle part of the slope, facing south, was an enormous dark cave mouth, some three hundred yards above them.

Amelia clutched Jamie's hand again. Everyone had stopped dead in his tracks: Seventy pirates stood in groups of six or seven, scattered across a broad line of march, staring with frank wonder and fear at that dark opening.

Even Captain Deadmon seemed subdued. "There it is," he said at last. "Let's fall back a bit, lads, and plan our strategy for the final assault."

"Stop doing that," Jamie whispered to the princess, trying to free his hand from her grasp. The seventy-odd others clustered in the deep shade beneath a tall oaklike tree, and from them came a murmur of contending voices. "You're acting just like a girl," he said to her.

She blinked her brown eyes at him. "But I *am* a girl."

"Well, you don't have to behave like it, do you? Now leave me alone. We have to plan an assault, and that's man's work."

Amelia's lower lip trembled, and she turned and walked away. For a moment Jamie felt guilty, but the men were deep in their plotting, and he hurried to join them. "An open attack?" tattooed Mr. Caulker was saying. "Risky, Cap'n, very risky."

"I'm for the guns," explosive Mr. Fletcher, the gunner, said in his volatile way. His drooping gray mustache fairly bristled with his enthusiasm: "We could take the pinnace back, unship a couple o' fourteen-pounders, and warp them around to yonder bay." He pointed, and for the first time Jamie noticed that there was indeed a shoreline not far from them, a few hundred yards down through the trees. "With my magic, we could bombard the cavern until we drive 'im out—"

"No, no," roared Crispin, a sun-darkened man who was normally the most silent member of the crew. "Where's the glory in that? Me for a straight fight, man against lizard, hand to hand—"

"You're for dinner, you mean," put in another. "Crisped Crispin, piping hot!"

Jamie, boiling with impatience, listened to the debate for as long as he could stand it, and then he went back to the clearing to look at the cavern opening, mysterious and beckoning. He saw a flash of color there, something yellow, gone in an instant. Had it been the dragon?

He glanced back at the men, but their discourse was as heated as ever. *I'll just climb up a little way,* Jamie promised himself. He ascended the easy part of the slope until he was halfway to the cavern opening, but still he could see nothing. Jamie worked one of the little pistols out of his belt and put it at half-cock. He looked behind him and saw that the men were now hidden under the eaves of the forest. *Just a few more yards,* he promised himself, and he climbed again.

He reached the very lip of the cavern. The tunnel looked cool and dark, with a floor of clean gray sand, very dry and loose, and Jamie shivered as he saw there tracks that might have been made by some gigantic bird. Dragon spoor, he thought.

And then he noticed something else: the print of a shod human foot. A print that, in fact, might have been made by—

"Princess Amelia!" Jamie said with a gasp. He thought of the glimpse of yellow he had caught—and remembered that the shirt she wore was that identical color. The silly girl had wandered right into the jaws of the waiting dragon.

Jamie stood irresolute for just a moment. Then he muttered, "Blast the girl," in a voice that he tried to make like Mr. Pye's. Raising his pistol, he cocked the hammer fully and fired a shot into the air. He thrust the discharged weapon into his belt, drew the other one, and plunged ahead into the darkness of the cavern, hoping that the others were following him.

Jamie crept along with one on hand on the rough stone at his side, trying hard to peer through the gloom. The air grew cool and dry, and the boy felt his sweaty shirt clammy against his skin. Presently he saw a ruddy glow ahead. He tiptoed closer until he could see that it was a torch in a sconce chiseled into the stone itself.

But it was fifteen feet off the floor of the cave. No human hand had put it there. Jamie took a deep breath and hurried past, seeing another torch ahead and then another, descending into the heart of the mountain.

The passage had begun to bend to the left, and coming around the last turning, Jamie saw a brighter light ahead. The cavern opened out wider and taller, until suddenly it soared away on all sides—

And there was Amelia.

The princess sat in an ornate wooden chair pulled some distance away from a fireplace. Beyond her, he could see shelves and perhaps more furniture, but firelight dazzled him. At any rate, she was not facing him, but was in profile to him. He rushed toward her. "You certainly—" he began in an angry voice.

"Oh!" Amelia looked around, her eyes wide. "Here he is now!"

And from his right Jamie heard a sudden inrush of air. It was not wind, or smoke flying up the chimney. It was something he had never heard before, and yet instinctively he knew what it must be.

It was the sound of a dragon breathing.

CHAPTER 12

Gravis the Gray

Jamie whirled, raising his pistol. "No!" cried Amelia

"Run!" he screamed, aghast at the size of the creature before him.

Someone pushed him hard between the shoulder blades, and Jamie fell to his knees, the pistol flying out of his grip. "Don't you dare!" Amelia yelled. "You're scaring him."

"Make it go 'way," said the dragon, a great scaly blue-gray creature.

"He won't hurt you. He's sorry." Amelia glowered at Jamie. "Aren't you?" She gave him a painful kick on the left ankle. "Tell Gravis how sorry you are."

"Is he—is this—" Jamie stammered.

"This," Amelia said, "Is Gravis the Gray Dragon. He had just started to tell me about himself when you came charging in." Amelia's head came up to the dragon's waist. She patted its knee reassuringly. "There, there, Gravis. Jamie won't hurt you. He's only a potboy."

Jamie's face felt hot. "I am not!"

She gave him a glance of deep contempt. "Well, he's only a cabin boy, then. And he *can* be rather nice when he wants to be."

The dragon's voice was high-pitched for the creature's size: "But Captain Drake assured me that if I made all the winds of the world welcome here no one would ever find my little island."

"Well, you see, Jamie has a magic wind talent of his own," Amelia said. "Here, take this." She gave Gravis her handkerchief. "Now wipe your eyes." Gravis did his best, though the handkerchief turned brown and flaked away.

"Oh, no," the dragon sighed. "Look what I've done."

"No, that's all right," Amelia said.

"Very kind," sniffled the dragon. Another tear rolled down its cheek and fell to the stone floor, where it hissed and bubbled and ate a little pit.

The chamber was most odd. It did have human-sized furniture, a table, chairs and a large assortment of sea chests, but there was a bulky shapeless something against the farthest wall, and a table that was six times human-size, and shelf upon shelf of—

"Books!" Jamie cried.

"Oh?" Gravis said, sniffing in a final tear. "Do you like reading?"

"Me? No, not really. But you—"

"I adore reading," the dragon said. "Reading maketh a full dragon, you know. As soon kill a man as kill a good book, for he who kills a man kills a reasoning creature, but he who kills a book kills Reason itself. I read that somewhere."

"You've got thousands of them," Jamie said. Some of the books were huge brown leather-bound folio volumes with black iron hinges, some were small gray paper-bound sextodecimos, and there were all sizes and shapes of books in between, cloth-bound, board-bound, and slip-cased. Every shelf sagged under the weight of all their accumulated learning. More piles of books flanked the bookshelves and made a maze of the farther parts of the lair.

"Yes. I've imported them over the years. I've collected gold from shipwrecks—"

Jamie's head spun. "Gold," he murmured.

"Yes," said the dragon, looking faintly distressed. "Sometimes a treasure ship will come to grief on a sand bank or on a coral reef and will be deserted, and since the gold is doing no one any good in the hold of a stranded ship, why, I take it. Salvage, that's called. And then I fly to a civilized country and use the gold to purchase books—anonymously, of course, for most tradesmen are prejudiced against dealing with dragons, but there are ways—"

Jamie asked, "How much gold do you have now?"

"Now? Right this minute, you mean?" The dragon scratched his head just behind his left horn. "Well, dear me, I'm sure I should know that. Let me see ... Hmm. Yes, I believe that right now, as of this moment, I have a grand total of nothing."

Jamie sat down on the bare stone. "You have only these—" He waved his hand at the thousands of volumes.

Amelia said helpfully, "They're called books, Jamie."

"But why?" Jamie asked.

"Oh, I was just telling Miss Amelia that," the dragon said. He had gradually relaxed and now lay full length on the floor. His body was about the size of an enormous bull's, his tail another eight feet or so, and his neck about six feet long.

"I will not deny that I used to be just a typical dragon, doing typically dragonish things. You know the usual lot: burning villages, kidnapping maidens, incinerating knights errant, that sort of nonsense. But one day while I was resting in my cavern, I overheard some village boys talking. 'That's where the dragon lives,' said one. 'What does he do?' said the other. 'Eats people,' said the first. 'Why?' said the second. 'Who knows?' said the first.

"Now, to begin with, that was just *wrong*. I've never eaten a human being in my life. I've snacked on sheep and goats and the odd pony or two, but humans? Never! But I confess that the boy's question bothered me: Why? Why did I do the things I did?

"I honestly did not know. I was a very young dragon at the time—this was six hundred years ago, you understand—and had not spent much time in introspection. But once the question took hold of my mind, it was awful, really. Why did I do the things I did? Why did any dragon?"

"Gravis is a philosopher, you see," Amelia said.

The dragon nodded. "Alas, but at that time an untutored one. My parents assumed I would be an ordinary dragon and never bothered with my education. When they turned me out of the nest,

my dad said, 'Go forth, Gravis, and pillage proudly.' But now I want to be more.

"Well, that called for learning. I flew to Uxbridge and kidnapped a don—"

"Kidnapped a don?" exclaimed Jamie. "You stole a *teacher*?"

"Only a little one," the dragon said, looking sheepish. "I took him to my cave and showed him the piles of gold and jewels I had accumulated. I promised he should have them if he would educate me."

Jamie rested his chin on his hand. "You *wanted* to be educated?"

"Certainly. How else was I to answer the questions in my head? At any rate, the kind Dr. Anselm consented, and we had a most enlightening four years together. I learned to read fast as anything, and before long we were doing classical languages, philosophy, and disputation. At the end he conferred upon me an honorary bachelor's degree, and I gave him my entire hoard. And then I flew the world over to find a spot where I could continue my work in private. Happily, I chanced upon the island."

"He's made it his home ever since," Amelia said. "And he's done wonders with it."

"Thank you, Princess," said the dragon with a graceful curving of its neck, rather like a six-ton swan. "I know the place is a bit ascetic, but then that suits a scholar's taste. Yes, I sought solitude for my independent study. I was still trying to answer that question: *Why?*"

Jamie said, "I suppose you don't even breathe fire?"

"Of course I don't. I let my dragon-fire go out ages ago." Gravis opened his mouth wide and exhaled hard, stirring Jamie's hair. The dragon's breath smelled of cinnamon and cloves. "Not a flicker."

Jamie waved away the moist air. "But Captain Deadmon thought—"

"Anyway," the dragon continued, ignoring him, "I lost myself in research. By now the question had become generalized: Why are dragons dragons? Might they change? Or are they fated by cruel fortune to live lives that make them cursed and feared by all? I labored alone until about a hundred and fifty years ago or so, when a ship of Anglavon discovered my island.

"Because of my tutor, I have a very soft spot for the folk of Anglavon, and so I came out to greet the ship." Some of the scales on the dragon's head bristled outward in indignation. "They were terribly hostile, and they even fired their guns at me. So I grabbed the first one I could reach right off the deck and flew him here to my cavern to teach him some manners. And who do you think it was?"

"I don't know," said Jamie hopelessly.

"Why, Captain Edmond Drake, of course. He professed himself ready to die in single combat with me. Nonsense, I told him, and then he began to listen to me. Such an understanding fellow. After we became friendly, I told him where he could find the Zampian treasure fleet and he patched up all our differences with his crew. He also gave me a way to keep my island safe."

"This is the magic part," said Amelia.

"Indeed it is," agreed the dragon. "You see, his navigator had the magic of talking to the winds. He called all the winds of the world here. Using him as an interpreter, I gave them this island as a place to rest when they were tired of blowing, and in gratitude they agreed to whisk away any visitors. Up until now it has worked."

"Jamie has wind magic of his own," Amelia said. "It's better than Nanny's magic, even. Oh, Gravis, tell Jamie about the book you've written."

"Oh," said the dragon with a modest cough, "it's nothing much. Here, let me show you." It rose, stalked to the huge table, and took from it a bundle of papers some six feet long by four wide. These it dropped with a dust-raising crash. "I have to order the paper specially made," explained Gravis.

The stack of creamy white pages came up to Jamie's knees. He stood on shaky legs and read, in much distorted perspective, the title, written in an old-fashioned handwriting and in letters six inches tall:

On the Reputed Evil of Dragons:
Is Society to Blame?
An Enquiry into the Behaviour
of Pyretic Reptiles
by Gravis the Gray
A.B. Uxbridge (Hon.); *Draconis Majoris* (Ret.)

"A book," Jamie mumbled. "You've surrounded yourself with hundreds and hundreds of books, and you're writing another one."

"Well, yes," said Gravis. "And I flatter myself that it is the first truly comprehensive work on the subject done by a scholar of my species."

"Isn't it wonderful?" asked Amelia, touching Jamie's hand.

"Don't do that," Jamie scolded. "Not in front of a dragon. Don't you see what all this means to Captain Deadmon? To the others—"

At that moment a great clattering arose from the passageway. Jamie spun as half a dozen sailors came spilling into the chamber, their eyes wide and their cutlasses drawn. "Oh, my stars," moaned Gravis. "More guests!"

Squok fluttered in, caught sight of the dragon, and pulled up short, treading air. "Awk!" he cried, sounding like a parrot for the first time since he had left the inn with Jamie. "Dragon dead ahead!"

Gravis squeaked in alarm, turned, and crept into a side passage until just the tip of his tail showed. "No!" Amelia shouted. "Put your weapons away. You're frightening him!"

"Frightening who?" Sharkey asked, and Jamie realized that the men had not even noticed Gravis.

"Dragon!" squawked Squok, but his voice was drowned out by someone bellowing, "Make way! Make way for the injured there!"

The privateers shuffled aside. Jamie cried out at the sight of

Mr. Border supporting Mr. Pye, his head wrapped in a bloody bandage.

"Hello, lad," muttered Mr. Pye with a wan smile. His dark blue eyes had gone pale, his face white. "Out of the frying pan and into the lair, eh? Curse Hawke!"

"Hawke?" Jamie asked in confusion.

Captain Deadmon had joined them. "Everyone safe? No dragon, eh? Just my luck—"

"There he is!" screamed Squok. "Hiding, the scurvy reptile!"

"Shush," Amelia told the bird with a stern glare. "Captain, there is a dragon, but he's friendly."

Deadmon stared at her with his fixed gaze. "A friendly dragon? I suppose that would just be the type I'd run into. How is my first mate?"

"Not in a good way. And dragon or no," the surgeon said, "I need some things. Who's got my bag? Fetch it here. Someone boil some water. Let's get Mr. Pye before the fire yonder and make him comfortable. That cut will need stitches."

Jamie asked, "Doctor, what happened?"

"What happened?" Border said, unpacking his case. "Why, that cursed Roger Hawke followed us into port. That scurvy dog stole your good wind, and his black-sailed frigate crept right in behind us, in the dark of night, when we couldn't see. His men have captured the *Betty* and are holding hostages."

"Mrs. Llewellen?" Amelia asked, sounding stricken.

"Aye, lass, and the three guards. Hawke sent a deputation to us, Mr. Pye went to answer them, they exchanged a few words, and before we knew what was happening, one of Hawke's men drew his sword on Mr. Pye. Mr. Pye gave him back blow for blow, but he took a nasty gash on the forehead." Border held up a lancet, a needle-case, and a box and nodded. "Aye, this is what I need."

"Water's ready, sir," someone called from near the fireplace. Many of the sailors had shucked off their jackets and had made a sort of bed for Mr. Pye.

"Let me see what may be done," Mr. Border said. "Jamie, bring the case. I may need other instruments."

Before they reached Mr. Pye, a far-off booming sound, like distant summer thunder, interrupted. A second later the whole mountain shook. Small rocks and pebbles fell from the invisible high ceiling and clattered to the stone floor all about them.

"By the Powers!" Deadmon said. "Hawke is bombarding the mountain itself!"

# CHAPTER 13

Defeat!

Jamie stayed with Mr. Pye while the doctor patched him up. The boy gasped at the sight of a three-inch saber cut on his friend's forehead just above the left eyebrow and had to grind his teeth together as he watched the surgeon sew the gash closed with neat, small stitches. Mr. Pye lay conscious but uncomplaining, wincing at each stitch without crying out.

When at last the operation was done, Mr. Border looked into both of his eyes, held up first two and then five fingers for Mr. Pye to count, and at last pronounced himself satisfied. "You'll do. You may have a scar, but you'll recover."

"The ship?" asked Mr. Pye.

"Taken," Border said.

"And Clara a prisoner!" Mr. Pye raised himself on his elbow. "We must—" he fell back, gasping.

"You're far too weak," Border said. "You need—"

"Brandy?" asked a tremulous voice.

Border started. The dragon had crept out. "I have a nice keg of brandy that washed ashore last year."

Border, like all the other men, stared at Gravis with stark astonishment. "Brandy would be fine," the doctor murmured. "In fact, I wouldn't say no to a glass myself."

"Don't attack him," said Captain Deadmon. "Steady, lads."

Gravis went into yet another side passage and returned with

a keg clenched between his jaws. He set it down carefully. "And there's this," he added, using one of his forepaws to present a tiny package to Border—the package was tiny for a dragon, that is; it was about the size of a small book. "Medicinal herbs, very soothing. Make a poultice of these and bind it to the man's head, and it will speed healing and prevent a scar from forming."

Border opened the bundle and sniffed at the dry green leaves inside. "They have a wholesome fragrance. I'll do as you say. Jamie, get a gill or so of brandy into Mr. Pye, if you please."

Jamie tapped the keg and, supporting Mr. Pye with an arm around his neck, did indeed get a little of the fiery liquid into the first mate. Mr. Pye's color improved. "There," he said. "That's better. Hello, dragon."

"You may call me Gravis," said the dragon, sounding pleased. "And I have the honor of addressing—?"

"Andrew Pye," Jamie said. "First mate of the *Betty*."

"And a wonderful poet," added Amelia.

The dragon clapped his forepaws together. "A poet! How marvelous! Tell me, sir, which side do you take in the controversy of the Ancients versus the Moderns? I myself incline to the view of Progress as the determining factor in—"

"Not now, please," said Mr. Pye. "We must recapture the ship."

Amelia explained to the dragon: "Pirates have taken the *Betty*. And my Nanny is aboard, and a prisoner." Another volley thundered outside, and more debris rained around them. "They're firing guns at your cavern now."

"Why, the horrid things," the dragon huffed. "Someone just go tell them to stop that at once."

But there was no one to send. As the day wore on the pirates did not cease their bombardment, though the worst they did was to topple a bookcase. "My Natural Sciences section!" wailed Gravis. After conversing with the dragon, the captain fell into a deep depression and stood in a corner, speaking to no one, not even Squok, who stayed on his shoulder crooning solicitous remarks.

Once their initial fear and suspicion had worn off, the crew worried more about the pirates outside the cavern than the dragon inside. On Mr. Caulker's orders they established a guard at the cavern mouth, armed well enough to resist any attempt to storm the lair.

Toward afternoon the captain called his officers together and addressed them: "Men, I have brought you on a fool's mission. We have found a dragon's hoard, all right—but it is a hoard of books. Hawke has taken our ship and holds as hostages three of my men and my passenger, Mrs. Clara Llewellen. The pirates outnumber us at least three to one. I see nothing for it but to sue for terms."

Mr. Pye, recovered enough to sit up, scowled. "Strike our colors, Captain? I've never heard you suggest that before."

Deadmon put a hand on his first mate's shoulder. "Aye, sir, but we've never been caught in a dragon's lair before, either."

"Sir!" Jamie said. "Let's ask the dragon to help us."

Deadmon looked uncertain. Squok said, "Sign articles with a crawling lizard? Never, by thunder!"

"Hush," said the captain. "It isn't regular, but then neither is the situation. Go, sir, and see what you can do."

"Aye, aye," said Pye.

Jamie gave him a hand, for Mr. Pye was still weak and unsteady. The dragon lay curled against his bookcases, holding them firm against the vibrations of the bombardment. "Barbarians," Gravis said with a sniff.

In a few words Mr. Pye sketched in the villainy of Hawke, the dragon looking more and more upset as the full tale unfolded. "And so," Pye concluded, "we beseech your help, sir. If you will fight on our side against Hawke—"

"Say no more," begged Gravis, averting his eyes. "Never! I cannot."

"But why not?" Jamie asked.

"That," said the dragon, gesturing dramatically at the huge stack of manuscript, "is why not. I have just finished an epic study of the sources of draconic evil, and have come to the conclusion that a pacifistic dragon is a possibility. To engage in violence would wholly vitiate my point."

"Oh, please." Amelia had joined them during the last of Mr. Pye's recital. "Those terrible men captured my Nanny. Though I'm not fierce, I'm sure I'd fight for her."

From across the cavern, Captain Deadmon called out: "Mr. Pye, I want you."

With a hasty bow, Mr. Pye left them and made his way over to the captain, gingerly enough but at least with more steadiness than he had shown earlier.

"Look at him," Jamie said. "The pirates have hurt him, and he still is full of fight and fury. Surely you can bring yourself to help out such a good man."

Gravis looked more and more miserable. "But I can't," he said. "Though the cause is just, I haven't anything to fight pirates with. My fire is out! And what is a dragon without fire?"

Squok landed on Jamie's shoulder. "A big useless lizard, is what," he said. Jamie shushed him.

"Your chicken is right," moaned the dragon.

All of Squok's feathers stood on end. "Chicken? Chicken? You great overgrown garden toad, I'm a parrot."

"I beg your pardon." The dragon reached to the top of the enormous table and retrieved a greatly oversized pair of spectacles, pince-nez, which he clamped onto the bony ridge of his snout, magnifying his already huge eyes. "I've always been a bit farsighted," he apologized. "Really wonderful for spotting prey at a distance, but not so good for clearly making out small print or small birds. Now I see you are indeed a fine specimen of the *psittacidae*. Do accept my apologies."

"Gravis," pleaded Jamie. "Forget the parrot. Will you please help us?"

But the dragon only sighed. "I am truly sorry. But without my fire, I am nothing—" the boom of guns and the vibration of impact broke off Gravis's statement, and again small pebbles showered down on their heads.

Just then Deadmon called Jamie over, and he left Gravis still talking to Amelia. "Yes, sir?" the boy asked.

Deadmon's face was shadowed, averted from the light of the fire. "Jamie, I have asked Mr. Pye to go out under a flag of truce. Will you go to steady him?"

Jamie's heart sank, for he remembered all too well the vile hold of the *Flying Terror*. But he tried not to show his dismay. "I'd be proud to stand by his side."

Deadmon's voice was kindly: "I'll not deceive you, lad. There may be treachery on their side, and if we lost Mr. Pye and you, we would lose an injured man and a boy. Do you see?"

Of course. If it came to an all-out fight, Deadmon would need sound sailors, not wounded men and youngsters. "I understand, sir."

"Then go with my blessing. Wicks, is the flag ready?"

Mr. Wicks had fashioned a rude flag of truce from someone's white shirt. Jamie took it.

Deadmon put his hand on the boy's shoulder. "Watch for treachery, lad. And you might as well have this. I found it on the floor." He passed over to Jamie the little pistol that the boy had lost earlier. With a blush Jamie accepted it and thrust it into his belt.

"Let's go." Pye sounded brisk enough, but he had to rest twice during the long walk out of the tunnel. The men at the cavern mouth reported that Hawke's crew had encamped all along the beach. After lowering all sail to keep the vessels safe from the winds, they had towed the ships from their safe anchorage to this more open bay, and both of them now stood offshore.

Mr. Pye murmured, "Come, Jamie. Let us see what this Hawke has in his talons."

They stepped into the mouth of the cavern, Jamie waving the flag of truce. From there he could see the *Betty* anchored in the bay, and just beyond it a much larger frigate whose furled sails were jet black. Flying from her foremast, a Jolly Roger whipped in the offshore wind.

Dropping his gaze to the beach, Jamie saw that it was thick with men. Hawke's men had set up four long guns, their muzzles aimed at the mountain. One gun crew waved a white flag in response to their own. "Come, lad," said Mr. Pye, leaning on Jamie's shoulder. "Keep a weather eye out for gales."

They struggled down the slope. Six or seven pirates stepped out from the trees at the foot of the mountain. "This way," one of them growled, and they followed him.

A campfire blazed in a small clearing, and beside it stood two men. One of them was easily six-and-a-half-feet tall, with a great tangled red beard and a fierce nose. He was a stranger, but Jamie knew the other man in an instant: Walter Creighton, the former master of the *Flying Terror*.

"Here they is!" he stormed. "Let me touch 'em up with Adder, Cap'n, do." He drew a long sword.

"Put away your weapon, fool," purred the taller man. He doffed his broad-brimmed black hat with mock civility, and the single white plume decorating it bobbed with the motion. "Do I recognize Mr. Andrew Pye, late of the *Bouncing Betty Bowers*?"

"You do, sir," Mr. Pye returned coldly. "There is no need to introduce yourself. The world is well acquainted with the visage and figure of Roger Hawke."

"You talk like a chaplain," Hawke said. "That was a grand device you played on my lieutenant. The Black Spot indeed!"

Creighton growled.

"We have come to discuss terms," Mr. Pye said. "I see no need in extending the interview beyond that."

Hawke's smile was grim. "Very well: Here are my terms. My men had taken rightful plunder, to wit, a princess and her governess. We have the governess already stowed safe below hatches aboard our vessel, along with her brave bodyguards. I want, and I shall have, the princess as well. So that's article one of my terms."

Pye nodded. "I shall tell my captain."

"Aye," said Hawke with an oath. "Tell the animated skellyton! And tell him that I have his ship, and I mean to keep her." He grinned again. "O' course, I'll have to change her name. *Bouncing Betty* indeed! But she's mine now, and that's flat. That's article two."

Pye nodded again. "And our crew?" he asked.

Hawke said, "Four of you've cost me a pretty ship, and the four must be turned over to me for punishment. We may feed you to the sharks, or we may sell you as slaves. The rest may rot away here on the island for all of me. And that's article three."

Creighton stirred, but Hawke raised a silencing hand. "As for article four, why, 'tis well known that Deadmon sought a dragon's hoard, and here he's found it, or I'm much mistook. Your men will just undertake to bring me the head and hoard of that there dragon."

Pye shook his head. "Impossible. This dragon has no hoard worth speaking of—"

"Liar!" thundered Hawke. He drew his cutlass. "A dragon with no treasure! Think I'm a baby, do ye? His head and his treasure, say I!"

When Hawke fell silent, Pye said, "Very well. I'll return to the captain and—"

Hawke stroked his long red beard, his eyes gleaming like silver nail-heads. "Avast! I nearly forgot him, your blessed Captain Corpse. That's the last article. He's to be turned over to me."

Pye's face froze. "To what purpose?"

Hawke roared, "To his rightful end! I means to chop him up and feed him to the fish. Then I reckon the name of Roger Hawke will be feared on every quarterdeck in the world."

Pye trembled, whether from weakness or from suppressed emotion Jamie could not tell. "Is that all?"

"Every last word, ye dog! Refuse that, and we'll blow your mountain to gravel!"

"Very well. Jamie, let's go."

The two walked away. During the climb, Mr. Pye paused frequently to catch his breath. "Sir," Jamie asked during one of these intervals, "will the captain accept?"

"No," Pye said shortly. "He'll never give up his ship. Besides, should Hawke carry out his threat—I mean if he should indeed chop the captain into pieces, as the villain is quite capable of doing—well, Captain Deadmon would become a wandering ghost,

137

lad. An unhoused spirit roaming forever, shut out of the next world and chained to this one until kingdom come."

Jamie shivered, thinking how awful it must be to be a ghost with no one to talk to and no hope of escape. "Then it's a fight."

Pye grunted. "A fight against deuced great odds."

They returned to the cavern. Deadmon stood before the fire, awaiting their return. Gravis and Amelia had retired to a far corner of the main cavern, where the dragon lay at full length, his head in the princess' lap as she stroked his snout and murmured to him.

Mr. Pye told Deadmon of Hawke's demands. Deadmon raised his head. "Impossible. I shall give Hawke a counter-proposal. If he will accept that, then so be it."

Mr. Pye gave his captain a searching look. "And what, pray, will your counter-offer be?"

Deadmon did not meet his eyes. "Why, I'll offer him myself. If he will forget the rest of his demands and leave you lads the boats from the *Betty*, then I'll give myself up."

"No, sir!" said Pye with vehemence. "I beg your pardon, sir, but that's no solution. Every man of the crew has signed on to follow you, to fight for you, and to be faithful to you, and we'll not abandon you now."

"Hear, hear!" shouted Mr. Border.

The crew cheered then, heartily, and Jamie realized that they had all been listening. Ned Sharkey sprang to his feet. "Give us leave, sir," he said, drawing his cutlass and brandishing it, "and we'll cut 'em down like pork! But never strike your colors, Cap'n, not for our sakes! We'd sooner follow ye to Davy Jones than another man to Paradise."

Deadmon's expressionless face melted into the semblance of a smile. "Men," he said, "I cannot tell you how full you have made my heart." He threw his head back. "Very well, then," he boomed. "If it's a fight Roger Hawke is looking for, let's accommodate him! May the Powers give victory to the right!" He turned to Jamie. "Lad, nip up the tunnel and tell the watch to fire one shot in the air as our answer to bloody Captain Hawke."

"Aye, sir," Jamie said, and he ran as fast as he could back up the tunnel. The men on guard seemed darkly delighted. One of them double-loaded his musket with powder but no ball ("For I've better use for my shot," he said grimly) and stepped to the opening of the cavern before firing.

The shot flashed and roared in the night. Immediately a scattering volley answered it. "Aye," growled the sailor, "fire away, ye villains! Waste powder and lead."

Jamie returned to the captain and reported what had happened. Deadmon nodded. "Get some rest now. We'll be up before dawn, and it will be a pretty trick to outfox those rascals, holed up as we are."

"I beg your pardon, sir," said the dragon. "I couldn't help overhearing your remarks, and if I may say so, there is another way out. I never use it myself, for it's very cramped for me, but if you will explore the western passage there—" Gravis moved his neck and pointed with his snout at an opening in the same wall as the fireplace—"you will find that it comes out a half mile north of the beach."

"Then that's the route we shall take," Deadmon vowed. "We'll leave three men at the mouth of the tunnel to convince 'em we're still jugged up. We'll leave one man with the princess to be her guard. The rest of us shall outflank Hawke's men and show them the fight of their lives."

Amelia, with the dragon's head out of her lap, got to her feet. "Please, Captain," she said. "May I name my own guardsman?"

Jamie frowned at her and shook his head, but she ignored him.

"Certainly," Deadmon said. "Whosoever you please, mum."

"Thank you," Amelia said with a smile. "Then I choose Mr. Timson."

Jamie turned to the captain. "Please, sir, no, don't make me. I want to—" he broke off in confusion. *"Barbecue?"*

"So be it," Deadmon said. "And now everyone look to your weapons and get your rest, for tomorrow we fight!"

Jamie slept little, and Mr. Pye found him wakeful before dawn.

"Here, lad," he said. "Take this." Jamie felt something hard thrust into his hand. He closed his fingers on the grip of a sword.

"A cutlass!"

"Yes—but try not to use it. Hawke's men have been in a tumble or two, and you'll find more than your match in any one of them. But you may need it for defense, so it's better you have one. Charge both your pistols."

Jamie hurriedly obeyed. Not a word was said about breakfast, and it was just as well, for he could not possibly have eaten a morsel.

The dark side passage was much narrower than the main entrance. The men groped their way along at a snail's pace, and Jamie more than once collided with the person ahead of him.

At length they broke out into the open beneath a starry tropic sky. "All right," the captain said as they huddled around him. "We march south along the beach, cross a low ridge, and that should bring us out on the left flank of Hawke's camp. Quietly now, boys, and smartly, for day's coming on fast."

They fought through tangles of underbrush as they crossed the southwestern peninsula, and then they were on sand again. The eternal winds, calm close to the central mountains, began to sough in the trees as dawn rose.

They came in sight of the bay. Both ships rode at anchor, with Hawke's turned broadside to the mountain, anchor chains fore and aft holding it steady against the insistent wind. Mr. Pye was breathing hard, but he had not fallen behind. "There they are," he said with a nod at the shore.

Jamie craned to see over some bayonet bushes. Sleeping pirates crowded the half-moon beach, and only one man stood, leaning on his musket and seeming asleep himself. Mr. Pye bent closer and whispered: "Stand by me, Jamie, for if we can, Wicks, Sharkey, and I mean to get to the boats yonder and try for the ship. We'll free her. By heaven, if the rogues have harmed her—"

"I'm sure the ship is all right, sir," said Jamie.

Mr. Pye gave him a peculiar look.

"Ready, lads," Deadmon said. He drew a pistol and fired it. With a yell the *Betty*'s crew stormed the pirate camp.

Jamie ran across the sand, and then a musket went off in front of him and he heard the ball whiz over his head. He pulled out one of his pistols and fired, to what effect he was never to know. A burly fellow came at him with a roar and a raised saber. Mr. Pye calmly raised a pistol and shot the fellow.

"Be more careful, lad," the first mate said, and then he whirled, raising his own cutlass to meet another foe.

Jamie stood back to back with him, a fresh pistol in his left hand and the cutlass in his right. Men cursed and shouted as blades hissed and clashed. At first Deadmon's crew had an advantage, for they had attacked with surprise on their side, but the superior numbers of Hawke's crew began to tell. Jamie saw Deadmon's men falling back on either side, fighting desperately.

"Retreat, lads!" came the well-known voice of the captain. Jamie looked in that direction and saw Deadmon standing like a rock amidst a raging sea: Fully ten men were on him, attacking, steel flashing. Deadmon made his own cutlass whistle wickedly as he warded them off, but clearly it was only a matter of time before he was overwhelmed. "Save yourselves, my hearties!" Deadmon shouted.

"The captain!" cried Mr. Tallow. "To the captain, or all's lost!"

Deadmon disappeared entirely from view as the pirates surged toward him. A green blur dropped from the heavens, struck one of the enemy over the head, and looped up again. It was Squok. "By all the winds of heaven!" the bird screamed. "I'll show you!" Squok reached the top of his arc and stooped again like a falcon, ready to strike.

An idea popped into Jamie's head.

He began to whistle.

CHAPTER 14

The Last Voyage

Jamie's cheeks bulged with the effort of whistling. In the turmoil no one except Mr. Pye noticed. "What's the tune, lad?"

But Jamie did not answer. He concentrated instead on the words:

> Sing ho! for a west wind, true and strong;
> The north wind, lads, is cold and drear.
> A south-east wind shall blow tonight,
> Sail before the eastern gale!

As the boy scrambled together every wind song he knew, the winds began to answer, tugging at Jamie's hair, dashing spray from the breaking waves. Mad whirlwinds appeared, dancing among the fighting men. Sand pelted Jamie's face, stinging like birdshot. More than one pirate cried out suddenly, dropped his weapons, and clasped his hands to eyes full of sand or burning salt spray.

"The wind fights with us, lads!" roared Pye.

Jamie whistled for all he was worth. Even as the boy watched, Deadmon fought his way free, his cutlass singing in the changing winds. The dismayed pirates fell back before his fury. A knot of them ran for the boats, but a waterspout snaked toward them, and they bolted into the woods.

"Thrash 'em, lads!" shouted big Ned Sharkey, picking up a

pirate in each hand and thumping their heads together with a sound like coconuts colliding.

The pirates faltered, broke ranks, and fled. It was over in a twinkling; the *Betty*'s men stood in full possession of the beach, the boats, and the discarded weapons of their foes.

"Victory!" yelled Deadmon, brandishing his cutlass. "Victory, by the Pow—"

The guns of the pirate ship spoke, drowning out his last word. An instant later the whole beach erupted as shot tore into it, and this time the *Betty*'s crew dashed for cover. Jamie, Mr. Pye, and Ned Sharkey dived behind a narrow outcrop of gray stone.

"Blazes!" Sharkey swore. "That ship carries ninety-six guns, and half of 'em's trained right on us."

"They couldn't all be manned," Pye snapped. "Two-thirds of Hawke's men were on shore. That would leave seventy on the ship. At four to a gun, they can hope to fire only seventeen."

Another broadside interrupted. They ducked behind the stone, and this time when they rose they saw that the shot had splintered one of the beached boats.

Pye said, "Hawke means to maroon us, and his crew into the bargain. We've got to get out there."

The pirates had in their confidence left four big guns and barrels of powder on the beach. "Sir," said Jamie, "if we could manage to swing those around, we could return fire."

Pye actually rose and took a step before Sharkey cried out, "Belay that! Asking your pardon, sir, but take a good look at Hawke's ship. Is that what I think?"

Pye sank back down, taking a sharp breath. Jamie made out a figure all in white standing on a kind of projection from the main deck of the black-sailed frigate—

"Clara!" said Mr. Pye.

"Aye, sir," Sharkey acknowledged. "We daren't fire."

Another cannonade raised a great spray of water close in to the beach. As the smoke cleared, Jamie saw Mrs. Llewellen desperately struggling to keep her balance. "Her hands are tied!" he said.

"Come with me, lads." Mr. Pye vaulted over the spur of rock

and ran for the beach. Sharkey and Jamie followed. Something green went tumbling through the air—Squok, making heavy work of flying in the contradictory winds that tore at the island.

Pye seized a small boat and moved it a foot or so before it stuck. "Help me here!" he raged.

With Sharkey on one side and Jamie on the other, they launched the little craft. Sharkey passed two oars to Jamie and then set his own two. "Pull, lads," Pye said grimly. "Pull your hearts out! And stand ready to back water when I tell you, or we're dead men."

Jamie put all his back into the task, and he scarcely felt Squok come plummeting into his head—but he felt the claws as the desperate parrot clutched at his scalp. "Ouch! Get to my shoulder!"

"Heavy weather, mates," screamed the parrot, but he got to Jamie's left shoulder and clung there.

The pirates fired again, and Jamie actually heard the rush of the balls overhead. They ripped into the beach, making kindling of a gig. "They've spotted us now," Pye said. "Get ready ... get ready...."

For a second Jamie thought the terrible sound he heard coming from the sky was another round of shot heading straight for him. Then a shadow passed over the boat. Looking up, he saw a flash of yellow belly scales and two enormous wings spread out like the pinions of a gigantic bat.

"It's Gravis!" the boy yelled.

"Now!" Mr. Pye shouted, and instantly Jamie reversed the direction of his pull. For a sickening moment the little boat seemed to stand on its bow. There came the explosion of the guns and almost simultaneously a drenching fountain of water.

"Thunder!" said Sharkey as the boat spun like a chip in a whirlpool. When it righted itself, it had reversed direction. Now Jamie saw the pirate ship only a few score yards away, and flying toward it the figure of the dragon.

And on the deck two of the swivel-guns swung up to meet Gravis's approach. "No!" Jamie shouted, knowing the dragon could not possibly hear. "You'll be—"

144

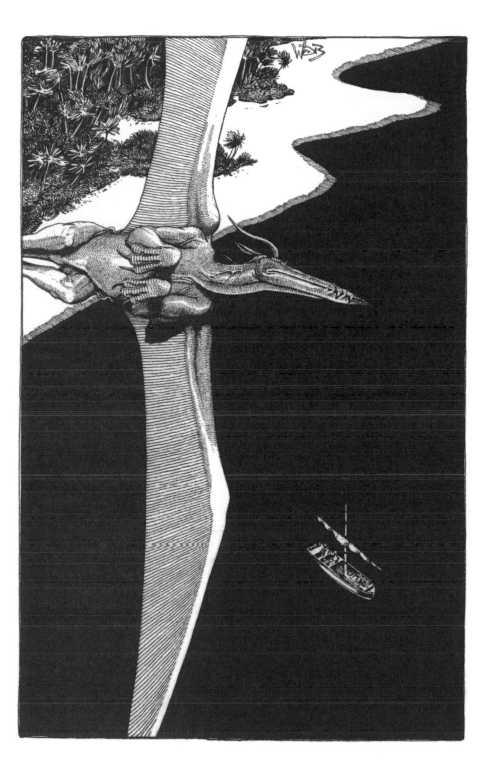

Both guns fired.

And from Gravis's gaping mouth came a blinding white flame. Two white plumes of steam appeared just ahead of him, and in a heartbeat he had sped through them harmlessly.

"Dragon fire!" shouted Pye. "He's vaporized the shot!"

Turning so that he passed the length of the ship with his belly toward the deck, his left pinion almost dipping in the water, Gravis swept down the craft from stem to stern. One moment Mrs. Llewellen stood on the plank, and the next the dragon had passed and she was gone.

The crew of the pirate ship leaped overboard in their eagerness to avoid social contact with a dragon. The few that could swim splashed and flailed toward shore, and the others sank.

The dragon made for the boat and actually hovered overhead while lowering Mrs. Llewellen. Mr. Pye seized her legs and eased her down. With a grin, Sharkey snapped his fingers, untying the rope binding her wrists. She threw her arms around Mr. Pye's neck. "Dear Andrew! You came for me. And you brought a tame dragon. How very clever of you!"

Gravis had made a wide circle, and now he was heading for the ship again. Two men, the tall red-bearded Hawke and the bear-like Creighton, had turned a Long Tom toward the dragon. Unlike the swivels, it fired fourteen-pound shot.

"They'll kill him!" Jamie cried out.

The dragon skimmed the water, making straight for the ship at incredible speed. Now he was half a mile away; now a quarter; and now merely yards—Jamie saw the flash of a match as Creighton made to ignite the powder at the touchhole—Gravis breathed that brilliant white incandescence again—And the cannon vanished in an explosion of white smoke. The dragon flashed into it and disappeared.

The smoke cleared. Of Hawke and Creighton there was no trace. The cannon had blown itself apart, and a huge chunk of the rail had gone with it.

And the dragon seemed to have vanished completely.

"Pull for the ship," Pye ordered.

With a sinking heart, Jamie rowed. Near the vessel floated a black hat with a white plume, the only sign they were ever to discover of Captain Hawke's fate.

Pye clambered up the side of the ship and tossed a line down. Sharkey helped Mrs. Llewellen up, then followed himself. Last of all came Jamie.

"Here they come," Pye said, waving his hat over his head. "This way, lads! The ship is ours!"

Jamie could not help staring at the great scorched, blackened section of the deck where the cannon had stood. It lay in scattered fragments of steel, and the railing had been blasted clean away for a length of ten feet or more. Despairing, he went to the port bow and gazed over the sea, searching the sky for some sign of the dragon.

"He's gone, Squok," Jamie said. "Gravis—he's gone."

"Gone fiddlesticks," grumbled the parrot. "There he is, plain as anything, under the water."

Jamie leaned over. "He's drowning!" He already had a leg up on the rail to dive over when the snaky neck broke the surface.

"Whoosh!" breathed the dragon, emitting billows of steam. "My, but spraying fire *does* make one thirsty!"

Jamie laughed until the tears ran down his face. "You can't drink salt water," he managed at last.

"You can," returned Gravis, "if you're a dragon."

In a matter of moments Deadmon and his crew had possession of both ships. A quick search produced the three guards who had been taken prisoner by Hawke, sound enough but angry at having missed the battle. No privateer was unaccounted for, though half a dozen had wounds serious enough to require the surgeon's attention. Deadmon dispatched Wicks and four more men to the island to bring back Barbecue and Amelia. Then the captain went to the bows and stood staring out at sea with an air of utter sorrow.

"What's wrong with him, sir?" asked Jamie of Mr. Pye.

Pye whispered back, "He's saved his crew and his ship, but he's failed in his main mission."

The crew roved over their new ship. "Know what this is, don't ye?" one of them asked another. "She's the *Royal Protector,* a naval frigate. Hawke took her last year off Dorchet, I hear."

Presently the shore party returned, with Barbecue, his crate of cookery goods, and Amelia safe and whole. Amelia and Mrs. Llewellen hugged and cried a little, and then Gravis, standing in water that came up to his shoulders when he stood rearing on his hind legs, leaned over the rail and begged to be introduced.

Mr. Pye performed the honors. "Clever trick, relighting your fire," he said.

"But I didn't," said Gravis. "You may thank the princess for thinking of a good substitute."

"Oh, no," Amelia said, tossing her auburn hair as she shook her head. "I only thought of it. The one who deserves credit is—"

"Me!" said the cook, coming close and inflating his chest. "Yes, me, Barbecue Timson! By gar, I knows how to stoke a hot fire, I does. A touch o' brimstone, a dab o' magnesium, a keg o' powder, and them big reading glasses o' his to focus the sun, and he had two explosive charges. Just enough, I'd say."

Squok had left Jamie to perch on Deadmon's shoulder. Now the captain came over, shaking his head. "Gravis, my friend, I owe you my thanks. You saved us all."

The dragon went blue-green with embarrassment.

"I have another task for you," the captain said. "If you don't mind."

"Oh, not at all," Gravis said.

"Then round up the scoundrels who are still on the island and let them know they have until sunset to clear out. If in that time they haven't taken to the boats and made off from shore, then say you'll track them down and fry their livers."

The dragon went pink. "Oh, I say. I won't *really* have to fry their—?

The captain winked.

"Oh," said Gravis. "I understand." He rose from the water with a clatter of wings.

For the next minutes Jamie watched him swooping over the southern peninsula and bellowing out the threat. A crowd of pirates came from the woods, dragged the surviving pinnace down, and Gravis hovered and held them until the boat was fully loaded.

Others, seeing the first crew away safely, rushed to the remaining boats. By midafternoon the last of them had passed over the reef, where the winds of the island had caught them and swept them out of sight. The dragon landed looking pleased with himself. "That's one hundred and seventy-one," he said.

"Hoy!" shouted a voice. They all turned. Mr. Tallow was staring down into an open hatch. "Look at this!"

Mr. Caulker and two or three others appeared. "Treasure, Cap'n," said Caulker, his tattoos glistening in the tropic sun. "Guldens, triploons, Vrenkish thalers—she's heaped to the scuppers with 'em. It's the biggest prize you've ever taken."

Deadmon shook his head. "Alas, it's nothing to me. I have yet to take a dragon's plunder and—"

"What!" squawked Squok. "You blind barnacle! Go take a look at the ship's bows, right this instant!"

They rushed forward. Leaning over the rail to look, the captain said, "The curse is lifted. I feel its weight slide from my shoulders and sink fathoms deep, praised be the Powers."

Jamie, also leaning over the rail, saw the name upside down. Perhaps the ship had once been christened the *Royal Protector,* but the imprudent Hawke had invited all the bad luck that had visited him by changing the name of his vessel.

It was now *The Golden Dragon.*

"I must go out with the tide."

That was the word Deadmon had spoken upon reading the name of the ship, and for the next three hours the men worked feverishly to follow his orders. First the *Betty* had to be emptied of everything usable, for Deadmon proposed to take that as his ship. *The Golden Dragon* he left to his men.

The crew fetched the cargo. Sharkey brought Jamie's bundle, and standing at the rail to receive it, the boy thought how carefully the sailor had guarded it ever since that day back in Pridden Town.

Deadmon walked the deck, his face serene. Mr. Pye appeared with Mrs. Llewellen on his arm. She had changed to a white lacy dress and really looked very handsome in the light of afternoon. With a broad smile, Mr. Pye led her over to Jamie and Amelia—who was again holding Jamie's hand.

Mrs. Llewellen looked flustered. "Ah, my dear. You are quite old enough now to live your life without a governess, and after all, your Grand Tour has finally ended. And so I—oh, dear, I don't know how to put it."

"Then allow me," said Pye. "I have done in earnest what Captain Deadmon once proposed in jest: I have asked Clara for her hand."

Mrs. Llewellen blushed. "And I have consented."

"Oh, Nanny," breathed Amelia. "I am so happy for you."

Mr. Pye left them for a brief conference with Captain Deadmon. They came back together, Deadmon shaking his head. "I shall be delighted to officiate," said the captain. "Only when you reach land, ma'am, be sure to have this rascal go through the ceremony again, before a proper parson. A captain can perform weddings, but I am not so sure about the legality of marriages done by dead captains."

The crew produced an assortment of instruments—a banjo, a harmonica, a trumpet, a concertina, a fife, and a drum—and played a sort of wedding march. Gravis, still deep in the water, looked on and shed tears that hit the ocean with a red-hot sizzle. Amelia was the bridesmaid. Jamie himself stood as best man, and when the time came he gave Mr. Pye a ring (part of the booty from *The Golden Dragon*) encrusted with enough emeralds to buy half of Great Camford.

They all cheered when at the end of the ceremony Mr. Pye kissed his new bride. "Will you be coming back to Laurel?" Princess Amelia asked.

With a fond smile, the new Mrs. Pye said, "No, dearie. Now that the captain is released from his vow, Mr. Pye is released from his articles and means to retire from the sea. We shall live in Great Camford."

"What?" Jamie asked, dumbfounded. He had assumed that Pye would take command of *The Golden Dragon*.

"Yes, lad," said Pye. "I've been amassing my share of treasure for three decades now. It's quite a sum. In the capital city of the realm, I shall set myself up in trade as a publisher. I shall publish precious slim volumes of poetry—"

"His own," whispered Mrs. Pye.

The first mate's smile broadened. "We shall see, my sweet. And I shall publish works of philosophy too, beginning with that fellow's yonder."

"Oh," said the dragon. "You don't mean it."

"I do," said Mr. Pye. "I couldn't sleep last night and had a look at your manuscript. Top-drawer stuff, really."

"And it's bound to be a success," said Mrs. Pye. "The first work by a real dragon? My dears, society will clamor for more!"

Gravis wasted no more time on false modesty, but rose from the sea and flew off to his cavern to fetch his manuscript. "But, sir," Jamie protested. "You can't just—I mean—after all, you know nothing about publishing."

"Ah, but I have a clever wife to inspire me," said Mr. Pye with a fond glance at the woman beside him. "Her magic is, that she makes everyone around her succeed a little better at what he loves. Why, Amelia wanted pirates and adventures, and she got them, did she not? And of course Clara moved me to produce my first new poem in ages. Anyway thirty years ago I knew nothing of privateering. If I have made a success of that, surely I can do the same with publishing. There cannot be *that* much difference between them."

A third of the crew was in agreement with Mr. Pye's notion of settling down. Mr. Border planned to retire to the colony of Gloriana, where a wife and family waited for him. Mr. Tattersall wanted to go back to his native village, buy the local pub, and keep certain boys who used to bully him out of the premises. Barbecue Timson glowed as he said, "With my cut of the swag, I'll set myself up in the job I always wanted—bein' a cook at a school for young people."

But the rest of the crew had no interest in retirement. Mr.

Wicks said that he had hardly begun life as an able-bodied sailor, and he'd be dashed if he'd give it up. Similarly, Mr. Caulker, Mr. Tallow, and Mr. Cutler were determined to follow the sea for at least a few more years, as were many others.

"But what about me?" Jamie asked, forlorn. "I wanted adventure too—and what am I to do now? Go back to the Pirate's Rest and ask for my old job as potboy?"

A heavy hand clapped him on the shoulder. It was Deadmon. "What do you want to do, lad?" the captain asked.

"Why—why, to have adventures," Jamie said. "To fight pirates and—and learn about the sea, and—"

"Sir," said Amelia from beside him. "I have an idea. Since so many of the crew want a ship, and a ship wants a captain, why not let Jamie have *The Golden Dragon?* The kingdom of Laurel needs a navy to protect us, and he could be Admiral Falconer—"

Jamie gave her a wild look. "That's crazy!"

"Not at all," came the stout voice of Mr. Caulker. "Why, he's a fast learner, we all know that, and we'd be glad to teach him. I say it's a grand idea."

And Mr. Wicks shouted, "Three cheers for Cap'n Falconer!" The ship rang with huzzahs.

"It's been decided." Deadmon reached a forefinger up to his shoulder, where Squok had been nuzzling his cheek. "Your orders, sir," he said to the bird, "are to accompany Mr. Falconer, see that he gets a good education, and keep him out of trouble."

"Aye, aye, sir," said the parrot in a birdy sort of whisper. He clambered from the captain's finger to Jamie's shoulder and perched there mournfully.

"You've given your word. Always remember, a promise is a promise." Deadmon gave the ship a long look around. "My lads," he said in a hearty voice, "I'm not one for flowery farewells. But I will say this: You've been the best crew ever a man sailed with; you've always done your duty; and you've made me blessed proud of you. Now Godspeed, each and all. Of a stormy night, when the wind howls, think of the poor souls at sea, and then spare a thought for your old captain, who found his berth at last."

The men on deck snuffled as Deadmon swung over the rail and dropped into a waiting boat. He rowed himself across to the *Betty,* climbed up her side, and cast the boat loose. He walked back to the wheel and took the spokes in his hands.

Deadmon glanced upward, and the sails unfurled themselves. Jamie heard a clanking as the anchor raised of its own accord and hung dripping at the bow. The sails filled, and the *Betty* slipped forward, heading for the west and the setting sun.

Jamie shaded his eyes with his free hand—Amelia had the other, of course—and watched the ship as it cleared the reef. Then he blinked.

The ship was rising.

Its barnacle-crusted bottom lifted clear of the surface.

A rush of air made Jamie look around. Gravis had decided to see the ship off. With his great wings beating hard, he flew side by side with the airborne craft for a long time before turning back. The *Betty* dwindled until she was just a tiny shining spark above the setting sun—and then she was gone.

The tropic night fell.

Someone—it was Tallow—asked, "What be your orders, Cap'n?"

Jamie realized that he had been addressed. "Why," he said, "get the ship ready, sir. We will catch the tide tomorrow morning, and then it's home to fair Anglavon."

"Aye, aye, sir," said Tallow, and he relayed the order.

Jamie looked behind him, but the dragon had returned to his cave. Mr. Pye and his new bride had gone below decks. Amelia too had left him alone, perhaps sensing how empty he felt. "Did I do right?" he whispered.

Squok shifted his weight on the boy's shoulder. "You can stand improvement, but I reckon that'll come."

For a long time the new captain of the *Golden Dragon* stood on the deck looking at the high stars of heaven. One of them, far to the west, winked at him. He winked back and went below to find a cracker for his parrot.